Merry Chr... May all your wishes come true!

Amy 8/11/04

New Shoes For Elizabeth

God bless you Elizabeth

American Book Classics™
An imprint of American Book Publishing
American Book Publishing
P.O. Box 65624
Salt Lake City, UT 84165
www.american-book.com
Printed in the United States of America on acid-free paper.

New Shoes For Elizabeth

Designed by Regina Zaslavskaja, design@american-book.com

Library of Congress Cataloging-in-Publication Data is available upon request.

ISBN 1-58982-155-6

Deason, Jenny Christine, New Shoes For Elizabeth

Special Sales

These books are available at special discounts for bulk purchases. Special editions, including personalized covers, excerpts of existing books, and corporate imprints, can be created in large quantities for special needs. For more information e-mail orders@american-book.com, 801-486-8639.

New Shoes For Elizabeth

By

Jenny Christine Deason

Dedication

For my father, Virgil Deason, who demonstrated to the five ladies in his life the meaning of unconditional love.

Preface

This book started out as a screenplay but my literary agent at the time suggested that the story should hit the market first as a book. If the book was received well, then maybe the screenplay could be placed. Thus I began the long process of re-crafting the tales of my family's oral history into book format. The handwritten manuscript was completed while working in Brussels. Three years later I am finally at this point and now am hurrying to finish a copy to share before the family reunion, the first weekend in August.

I am hurrying now because my mother has informed me that her aunt, the heroine, was ninety-two years old and in an assisted-living arrangement. Desperately I wanted to share this, her story, with her before my procrastination gene (fear-of-failure gene?) prevented that from happening. The family reunion would offer a wonderful place for this manuscript to shuffle among the relatives because I was far enough along in the process to be begging for critical comment. A few of my cousins also write. What better opportunity to get that much needed feedback.

But before you read the episodes reported here, please be advised that I have woven a fabric of fiction in order to blend separate stories into one tale. I have at times distorted the true timing of the events chronologically to knit as many of the family's stories as possible into one Christmas tale. Forgive me please for taking such literary license with the truth of our family's history.

The Huhn family that I remember was, and still is, a group of family-centered families struggling as we all do with the realities and burdens of life. The Huhn family members are winners, inventors, poets, mothers, fathers, preachers and teachers, engineers and lawyers, all having a common thread that ties us together—a family tree.

Introduction

I was four years old when I last remember sitting on my granddad's lap. He was in a wooden rocking chair on the front porch of the nursing home where he lived. Dutifully I was letting him rock me. Heck with that, I simply loved to be rocked. When I was two, I once rocked a rocking chair until I rolled it over. Grammy Huhn from then on had the chair propped up against her couch for fear that I'd repeat the incident.

But I sat calmly for Granddad, a scene rarely witnessed. He had me quickly occupied and asked me to count my fingers. Proud as I was at my accomplishment once finished, I pounced the "ten" count off the last finger and smiled up to get his applause and verbally did. But then Granddad demanded more.

"So, can ya count my fingers?"

I tried repeatedly but no matter how many times or in what direction I went, my count would stop at six. He encouraged me to check my work every time I ended his finger count at six. True to form I would get as upset as a rained-on kitten. I was sure that he was playing some kind of trick on me.

I would query why he only had six digits, which resulted in just more verification work for me.

"So count your mommy's fingers. How may does she have?" After following his orders I would report my findings back to Granddad by running noisily across the wooden planks of the porch. I had a talent for making the few feet of surface area to be crossed seem like an eternal thundering void to the sound-sensitive older occupants of the porch. But I was good at noise and I do believe that folks should do what they are good at.

"She has ten."

"And your daddy?"

My trip back across the porch had all but Granddad wincing in pain. He just smiled at the reactions of the other adults. They shook their heads at this bundle of rarely bridled energy. Granddad smiled too broadly; perhaps he was entertained as much by their pain as by my precociousness.

"He has ten, too." Granddad kept up the game until I had counted every finger on the porch. Every porch sitter had ten fingers except Granddad.

"So let me check your toes," I said as I sat down with a plunk and stripped off both my shoes and socks before Mom could even say the word "no."

"Yep, I checked 'em this morning and I still got ten. How 'bout you, Granddad?" I went to remove his shoe and that's when Mom wisely thought that the game had gone far enough.

My granddad was truly different. Years later, I would be told the story of how he became so different. You will also find a story about the only grudge that I knew my God-fearing and usually forgiving grandmother to bear. A grudge she bore until she died. A story about great greed and great generosity, all found in the shade of the same family tree.

Again, please forgive me the myths along the way. I hope not only to preserve some of my family's oral history but also to tell a compelling story. I would like to introduce you to a German immigrant farm family, the Burkhardt Huhn family from Seneca County, Ohio. The annual family reunion will find us again gathered on a farm near the seat of Seneca County: Tiffin, Ohio. I now take great pleasure in welcoming you into my family and a trip to another time. You only need to turn the page.

Jenny Christine Deason Tichenor

Chapter 1

The Journal

These words were found on the inside cover of Elizabeth Marie Huhn's diary:

To my dearest daughter,
For your thirteenth birthday, July 31, 1939.
May all your wishes come true.
God bless,
Love,
Mom

New Shoes for Elizabeth

August 1, 1939

Dear Star,

I thought about it for a few minutes and Justin and I wish on stars all the time. So if this is to be a journal of my wishes and dreams, then what better name than "Star." Mom gave me Star for my birthday. A journal costs a lot less than a pair of shoes. But I don't need a new pair of shoes until winter. My feet could grow by winter and then it would have been a waste of good money is how it's explained to me. Summer we all go barefoot almost all the time. It's just Sundays that are a problem. Mom won't let me, a girl, go to church barefoot. The boys are allowed to go barefoot to church until they are twelve, so only my older brother, Raymond Jr., has to wear shoes to church. That seems to be OK for my brothers. With five of them someone always has a pair to give to a younger brother. The older boys would clump around in Dad's old shoes if they have to. Sometimes Dad's shoes are two sizes too big even for Raymond Jr. But my feet are so much smaller than Mom's that her old shoes aren't even a possibility. I'd just walk out of them and she won't let me wear heels anyway. Not until I'm fifteen were her words on that subject. So, I have one pair of Mary Jane's that are two years old and two sizes smaller than I really need. Makes going to church a painful experience. One, my mom says, that is building my character. Poor little Chinese babies with their tiny feet all bound up are some of the visions that my shoe-wearing moments conjure up. My mind is always on my toes, not the sermon.

No offense to you diary—Star—but I'd rather that you had been a pair of shoes. Wishing upon a "Star" that shoes would be a Christmas present, since I don't have them for my birthday. And gifts only come around twice a year in our house.

Yours,

Elizabeth/Betsy

August 5, 1939

Dear Star,

Today was great. The church Ladies' Auxiliary (I had to ask Mom how to spell that) had a meeting in our kitchen to schedule the harvest luncheons. The farmers, the auxiliary ladies' husbands, have chosen the best week for the harvest activities using the Farmer's Almanac. The men have made a contract for a thrasher that they will share during the week. They will set aside some of their harvest money for next spring's seed account. That will leave the largest share of the profit to pay our annual rent for the land and the use of the thrasher. It's all a bit more than I can understand but I try. Seven farms will have the thrasher for seven days. That will require good weather the whole week and seven straight, incredibly long workdays. There was a debate about which farm would be tainted with the Sunday work. Straws were drawn. Thank heavens it wasn't our farm. You think God would forgive them one Sunday a year. We are farmers, for pity's sake. I'll pray for Daddy's forgiveness for breaking the sacred rules.

Our farm will be done during the middle of the week, on Wednesday. The men won't be totally worn out.

Once the days are chosen, the ladies plan the meals. My mom said that when men work that hard, they need a lot of food. Each lady is planning five chickens per day, two hogs for the week for fresh pork. We offered a cured country ham and the Oscars will kill one turkey. The McPhearson's had five rabbits to add and the Robertsons are willing to slaughter a calf. More milk for the family! Their cow had twins and they are willing to spare one now. I hate eating babies, but better that than have someone looking to put lamb on the menu, since my pet lamb is the only one in the neighborhood. Napoleon is safe for now.

Good night,

Elizabeth

August 12, 1939

Dear Star,

The older boys are such BOYS. I have five brothers. Justin, who is five, is the only one that you might even remotely want to get to know. Douglas is nine and Dad says won't see double digits if he doesn't straighten out soon. Jeffery made it to eight but by the skin of his teeth. Raymond Jr, my dad's namesake, is starting to act like a teenager, not a little kid. As far as I can see, it was about time, him being the oldest and all. Winston is seven and never would bother Justin and me on his own, but he goes along with Jeffery's ideas way too often. He and Jeffery are like bookends. Justin and I leave them alone. He and I usually go frogging or fishing at one of the creeks. If the big boys find us, we just run home at first sight. History has proven that we are to be the brunt of some sick prank if they get bored enough to seek us out.

Jeffery is especially devious; if he gets a bee in his bonnet, his eyes twinkle in a devilish way. A signal that has Justin and me running like the wind toward home.

I wish the boys had that bike they want so much. Maybe then they would have some quality distraction and Justin and I would be safe from their torments. In fact the bike might mean more to Justin and me than (can I even write it?) a new pair of shoes. Come winter though, I will probably regret having written that.

All for now,

Elizabeth

August 19, 1939

Dear Star,

For some reason as yet unknown to me, today feels special. Like someone's birthday, but it isn't. Why is it that some days just unwrap like an incredible gift? Today was one of those days. Late summer, beautiful blue sky, another Sunday. Since we aren't allowed to do anything that might even appear as work, I am not allowed to sew clothes for my dolls on Sundays. I use the quiet time of the day to write to you, Star. For some reason writing is not considered work—at home. Yet at school, it is. Who knows what rules really apply in God's mind? We humans are just struggling to comply with our own interpretations. Mom makes the boys redo last year's homework assignments during Sunday quiet time and that even has the word "work" in its name. The boys have pointed this out to Mom who says that that doesn't count. In their case it is a penance of sorts. Mom says the rule doesn't really count for children one Sunday, and then the next Sunday she refuses to allow us to do something considered fun to us, but work to her. It's these adult definitions that defy logic that determine the children's Sunday taboos. Milking cows is still done on Sunday and that's adult work. Somehow I'm not understanding God as well as I used to.

Shame on me for writing that on a Sunday even—God please forgive me for that infraction and I'll forgive you for ignoring my prayers for new shoes.

Unclear,

Elizabeth
August 26,

Dear Star,

Doug has a black eye and Mom wouldn't take him to church, so I got to stay behind to baby-sit him while Jeffery was drug off to church as part of his punishment for punching Doug. YEAH! A no-shoes Sunday! Doug of course wanted to play all morning rather than read the Bible with me as Mom and Dad had ordered. So I have time to write some before I start cooking the family lunch. Chicken and dumplings with carrots. I have my work cut out for me. Doug will be no help of course. At least the chicken has been killed, cleaned, and plucked. None of those are acceptable to me even though Mom fusses that some day soon I will have to prove myself in these tasks, too.

Maybe I'll find some cucumbers and onions in the garden and surprise Dad with his favorite salad.
Enough for now or I won't get my work done. Yes, it's Sunday, but somehow cooking doesn't count as work.

Elizabeth

September 3,

Harvest is next week. This time of year, I simply love being a farm kid. We don't go back to school until our farm is harvested. The theory is that we children can actually be of some assistance. Whoever made that rule didn't know my brothers. Got to go. Mom and I are canning tomatoes, making catsup and pickled beets. (Yuck!) Hot work on a hot day.

Elizabeth

September 4,

We dug the potatoes today. Well, not all of them, but enough to last the next few weeks. We'll let the balance rest until just before frost. Then we'll dig up the whole patch, they will be huge potatoes by then. Then we'll pack them into the root cellar in bushels filled with straw just like we pack away as many apples as we can. And the earliest of the apples have started to fall. I can taste the cider and apple pies already. From now until the snows fall we'll have apple cider for breakfast, lunch, and supper. Thank you, Johnny Appleseed.

Elizabeth

September 5,

Mom and I did an inventory of the pantry. Staples are getting low but she reassured me that the crop would pay the rent with enough left over to refill the pantry before winter. There was enough flour left to make the breads and piecrusts for the harvest day luncheon and then we'd buy two fifty-pound bags of flour with the crop money. That would get us through the winter lean months. Always has, even with five hungry boys to feed. Mom closed her eyes and prayed right after she had talked about getting through the winter. Sometimes she scares me. She worries so much. Each worry is signified by another prayer sent heavenward. She does that dozens of times a day lately. Should I be more worried than I am?

Elizabeth

September 6,

It is so hard to find time to write. But there is so much extra work to do around this harvest event that I am just so wound up when I go to bed that I can hardly fall to sleep. I'm writing after I go to bed with a bit of light that I can sneak on without alerting Mom. She'll want me well rested, for the next day will not be any easier than these last few. I should be so exhausted that I drop into bed. Yet here I am filled with thoughts that need to get out.

Today we stewed some apples for supper and saved some for the pies tomorrow. We canned again—apples, berries, jellies and jams—anything that sounded good when we thought about a cold winter's boring fruitless supper. I am so sick of canning. OH the pickles are ready. Which means two or three more days of canning after this harvest luncheon work is done. I think school is starting to sound good.

Elizabeth

Chapter 2

Harvest Home

September 6,

Dear Star,

Today is harvest day. That's all I have time to write today! Sorry. More later. It will be a busy day. Helping Mom
and trying to keep the boys outta trouble.

Elizabeth

P.S. It's 5 A.M.

Georgette wondered half to herself and half to the sink
in front of her, "What a perfect harvest day." Or maybe she

was talking to the pump as her arm worked it in an uncon-
scious rhythm until the pitcher was full. "Lord, please let
this be a perfect harvest luncheon." Her neighbors and
church friends bustled in and out of the wooden structure
that was home to the Huhn family. Georgette, Raymond,
and their six children called the tenant farm theirs for now.
Georgette and the other women fretted about the over-
bearing warmth of the kitchen as they performed the last
actions required to feed the harvest hands their main meal
of the day. Lunch. The cooking commotion was momentarily interrupted as every woman jumped at the sound of
thunder made by the slam of the kitchen door against its
frame, a noise that signaled the entrance of two of Georgette's brood. The two Huhn boys were spaced just far
enough apart that the entrance of each child was signaled
by its own heart-wrenching bang of the screen door. This
sound had become to the women—after nearly six hours of
cooking together in the Huhn kitchen—quite unwelcome. A
few of the helpers showed their major disapproval and
tossed annoyed glances in the direction of Georgette's
turned back. Heaven knows they'd never do so to her face.
Georgette seemed to sense the disapproval and responded
as if she'd seen their veiled judgments.

The Huhn boys had slammed the kitchen door so much
that Justin had thought its name was the *scream* door, since
he knew the sound of the door's slam was quite capable of
making his normally peaceful mother scream at his brothers. The name seemed fitting. Once he learned to read, he
did discover his mistaken understanding.

"Do not slam the door, Jeffery, do you hear me?" Georgette's mothering of the boys was not always what she wanted it to be. All those images of goslings obediently and willfully toddling behind a mother goose often made her wonder if God's nature was purposefully delusional to help humans "go forward and populate the earth." If she were a mother goose, her brood would not run under her wings in a thunderstorm, or be hustled wisely to the safety of the barn. No, her brood would more likely be running around with a key on a kite string, trying to prove that the Benjamin Franklin experiment the teacher had described was a hoax, another hoax perpetrated on them by that daffy woman the town had hired as their schoolteacher. Georgette laughed to herself, then smiled sweetly as she realized that at least two of her goslings would be dutifully nestled under her protective wing. Elizabeth would be there and Justin, the youngest, who rarely went more than a few steps from Elizabeth's side, would also be there. So a third of her brood could be counted upon to act with wisdom and intelligence. The balance of her flock was wildly out of her abilities to control. Sure she could try a small twig on their backsides, but they just laughed at her now. That approach had only worked when they were small. Now, the level of pain that seemed necessary to communicate authority, she was incapable of inflicting on her own child. Raymond Sr. was usually required for that degree of discipline. Georgette just tried to keep them from destroying themselves and others, and of course the farm. That seemed enough to expect most days.

The sons were wild ones, but her daughter was truly a gift from heaven. Georgette had called her Elizabeth. A great-grandmother's name was now her daughter's given name. Yet most of Elizabeth's schoolmates called her "Betsy," not Georgette. Georgette never used nicknames. She gave a child a name because that's the name she wanted them to be called. If she'd wanted Elizabeth to answer to "Betsy" she would have named her "Betsy"! Elizabeth was her only daughter—the second oldest and second mother to the younger boys and even a mother figure to Raymond Jr. when he wasn't thinking about it. As Georgette moved the pitcher of water into a set of helping outstretched hands, she unconsciously gave "thanks" for the assistance. Georgette absentmindedly repeated two gestures in quick succession. First she wiped her floured hands on the hip area of her apron. Her already flour-dusted hips were proof that this was not the first time that she'd used her apron and hips thusly today. Then swiftly she jabbed her right hand into the apron pocket to see if her dear husband had thought to leave her one of his "love gifts," as he called them. Sure enough, a small pansy had been left in her apron pocket. As busy as today was for him, he still managed to remind her that her efforts were appreciated. She placed the pansy back in her apron pocket. She wondered if her pillow would be likewise adorned. Her husband was still sweet to her, even after almost twenty years of marriage. Her hand released its hold on the pansy and then wrenched itself from the apron pocket and snapped open the oven door to remove two dozen more yeast rolls from the raging wood fire of the cast-iron stove. The sweet smell of fresh bread perfumed the kitchen. Georgette sniffed the air in delight and mouthed a "Thank you, Lord" to the ceiling for such a perfectly timed meal, as she placed the rolls on the kitchen table. Without a word being exchanged between the ladies, the pace of activity was doubled. The table was already laden with covered dishes waiting to be served. Though the table was at least ten feet long, one could hardly evidence the milk paint surface, it was so burdened with the foods prepared for the feast. Twenty pounds of potatoes, mashed and seasoned with chive and buttermilk, had been mounded into three bowls. Five pounds of candied yams, ten pounds of peeled sliced tomatoes, and cucumber and onion salad in vinegar dressing and one bowl of the same salad in a sour cream dressing to keep everyone happy, were also waiting. Pickled boiled eggs, deviled eggs, and every known combination of jelly and jam and butters sat next to the two mountains of sweet corn on the cob and baskets of rolls. The army of hands and feet started to move the feast outdoors and onto the tables in the yard. The second oven held the ham and the six chickens. These wouldn't be brought out until after the prayer was offered.

Another pair of women balanced additional stacks of corn on the cob on platters. One member of the two-women team defrocked the corn and plopped it into the boiling water of one pot while the other team member rescued cooked ears from a second pot and managed the ears onto a waiting platter.

The screen door jumped open again. The blur of two boys chasing one another up the stairs passed by so fast that they almost knocked over the carrier of the gravy bowl.

The carrier of this precious condiment artfully juggled her-self and the gravy through the onslaught of rowdies, but not without a furrowed brow and another stabbing glare at Georgette's back. Without turning around, Georgette chimed an apology, "Sorry for the boys, Wendolina." This seeming ability of Georgette's to react to unseen events surprised Wendy enough to wipe the furrows from her forehead in fear that this woman really did have eyes in the back of her head. (Georgette's children had often attributed this trait to their mother during Sunday school class discus-sions. Mostly the children seemed to be worried that God had the same excellent vision as their mother.) "Sunday school class volunteer Wendolina will never volunteer for this farm's harvest again," thought Georgette. Georgette tried to catch the last boy by the suspenders and reap some Judgment Day retribution on his hind end, a privilege deemed necessary for parents and teachers, police and vari-ous other government officials those days. Her random grasp came up empty again. Without missing a step, Geor-gette shifted her focus back to the whereabouts of the other children. Taking inventory of her brood through the kitchen windows she did "the count." Something she was no longer aware that she did. Out of the kitchen window she saw Justin and Elizabeth playing jump rope with Elizabeth's pet lamb. Everyone who knew of this pet trick wondered at such an animal-human connection that would cause a lamb to want to play jump rope to begin with, much less learn how to perform the trick as if for the sheer fun of it. Geor-gette wondered more practically how old the lamb could get before it started to taste like mutton. "I like lamb, but mutton is just too strong to eat for my taste." Once the thought had skipped through her mind, the shame of it followed right behind. "Elizabeth would never forgive me. Thank you, Lord, for providing us with enough food on our table so that lamb can stay a pet." Her thoughts paused for a brief bit of time and then she started her count again. "Well, that accounts for four out of six—two upstairs and…" At that moment her thoughts were interrupted by the heavy thumping of boys chasing on stairs, as the two children that had been the "upstairs count" dashed though the kitchen door. Of course they were again spaced apart just perfectly so as to allow the screen door one deafening slam per boy. While Georgette attempted to nab the last one, her reach was not sure enough and the scamperer made good his escape. Amazingly calm, she stood at the kitchen window and said out loud, "OK, that's four outside." She glanced out the back window to see the shadow of two small figures in the entrance to the barn. But weren't those two upstairs earlier? How did they get out to the barn without her hearing a door slam? She'd better investigate that later. That made the count six, which was the balance of the equation she had expected. Contented somehow by this simple math result, she went on with her meal preparations. Her actions continued as if the addition exercise had never interrupted her lunch planning. The satisfaction of knowing where her chicks were showed in the slight relaxing of the lines in her thirty-six-year-old forehead. Her forehead was creased deeply enough for a woman twice her age. These same creases again tightened as she turned to see all of her kitchen volunteers standing behind her, hands folded on the front of their aprons and eyes focused on the hostess, Georgette. They looked like troops waiting for the orders to charge up a hill. It was her house and the meal would be done her way. So the volunteers waited for her further directions.

"Alles richtig! (All right, then!)" she said in German with a slight smile of self-satisfaction, "let's ring them in." Georgette wiped her brow and her hands on her apron, walked out of the kitchen door, closed her eyes, bowed her head, grabbed the rope of the dinner bell, and "rang in the hands". She rang the bell once, waited three seconds, and then pulled the rope quickly three times. The men's heads popped up as backs straightened. Sleeves reached to wipe sweat from under their hats as the men lifted various coverings off their heads to allow a breeze to pass underneath. The faint machinery noises stopped as the men made their way from the field to the farmhouse yard. Some ran and some hopped onto a passing truck tailgate to ride to the lunch table.

Without a verbal command being spoken, the children came running, washed their hands at the side yard pump and started to carry food and pour iced tea and lemonade into glasses. A huge block of ice appeared from the icehouse and one of the women chipped ice with a pick while the children deemed to have clean enough hands by the chipper, carried the pieces to the glasses and plunked them in. Ice was a treat during the summer months. So of course, the children all popped a piece in their mouth first thing. Then Jeffery and Winston just had to put a piece of ice down Raymond Jr.'s back. This action took those three out of the helpful-hands lineup as they tussled on the ground.

Georgette yelled once to try to regain control but must have figured that her attention was better spent on the meal since Raymond Sr. would soon be on the premises. "Dad will make sure that these three don't act up again," Elizabeth reassured herself as Justin looked to her for a reaction. Elizabeth just shrugged and continued to help the ladies. Justin imitated her every action—he shrugged back and followed Elizabeth's steps to the chipper for another load of ice. Raymond Jr. now had both of his little brothers on the ground, one under each knee, and he was tickling them senseless. A scene that even had Georgette smiling at their antics. Well, at least until Jeffery reached up and popped Raymond Jr. in the nose. This was all it took to turn the event from horseplay into fisticuffs. After a few retribution blows on the younger two, Raymond Jr. ran to get a piece of ice to hold on his bleeding nose.

The two brothers, now set free by Raymond Jr.'s diverted attention, tried to look innocent the second they saw Raymond Sr. stalking them from the end of the driveway. Raymond Sr.'s eyes went steadily from one boy to the next. Raymond Sr. quickly assessed the situation and walked toward the trio as he unbuckled his belt. Terror painted the three boyish faces. Raymond Sr. may have only been four feet eleven inches tall, but to his boys, he was a mountain of a man.

Georgette, seeing the deliberate and focused approach of her husband toward her sons, concluded that her boys were in need of help. She strolled over to Raymond Sr. who didn't acknowledge her presence. His gaze never shifted from the panicked faces of his sons. The boys stood transfixed as if they were deer caught in headlights. Georgette touched Raymond Sr.'s arm and whispered so that only he could hear, "I would certainly support the need for discipline here except for Wendolina's heart condition, which might not withstand the sight of a typical bit of fatherly discipline. She simply might not understand, since she has no children of her own." Georgette paused to see if she was being heard through his rage. Sensing that she had gotten through his emotion and to his head, she pressed on. "And this might set a hard tone for the meal that is about to follow."

Raymond Sr. never took his eyes off Jeffery's returned stare during this wifely briefing, and just as certainly he never acknowledged Georgette's presence in any way. She had said her piece and she left his side for the table. She reached the table just in time to overhear Wendolina's remark to Josey, "Just like her to stop them from getting the beating they deserve. No wonder they're the little hellions that they are."

Raymond Sr. turned his back on the boys and placed his belt in its normal position. Calmly he headed for the pump where the other farmhands had been washing up for the meal, and he followed their lead.

Georgette walked over to the boys, arms filled with baskets of her freshly baked rolls, and instructed them, "You boys go wash up again and sit at your places." They grumbled in unison but obliged her, hoping that the punishment of sitting still until the end of the meal was as much retribution as their crimes would demand. No sooner had they washed up and started for their chairs as instructed, than brother Doug came out from behind the house where he had been waiting for his father's back to be turned to him. Doug made a break for Jeffery while Jeffery was focused on his dad's every move. Jeffery had reached his chair, as he was ordered to do, when Doug caught up to him and pulled down Jeffery's cutoff pants to expose Jeffery's worn and dirty underalls. Doug dashed away while Jeffery cursed, struggling to pull up his pants. All adult eyes were on Jeffery as he took half a step to pursue Doug, then thought better of it as both his dad and his mom had taken steps in his direction. Defeated, Jeffery sat down in his chair, head in hands. He was probably reflecting on the rude words he had just uttered. He knew that there would be some punishment for the curses he had shouted in front of the "church folk." Such an outburst would be talked about all over town.

Elizabeth shook her head in disgust. Justin gave a worried look to Elizabeth and squeezed her hand. Elizabeth acknowledged his concern with a helpless shrug yet reflected her own concern with her wrinkled brow. Elizabeth and Justin expected that Jeffery and Doug were both in for some days ahead when sitting down without pain would be hard to accomplish. Raymond Jr.'s nose was no longer bleeding, so he tossed the hunk of ice, which he'd been holding on his nose, in a backward hook behind him. The ice landed near Raymond Sr.'s boot as he stood chatting with a clutch of the churchmen, all of whom were staying dutifully out of the way of the womenfolk as the final preparations ran at full speed around them. Raymond Sr. eyed the ice, took notice of the blood, calculated a vector to determine the angle from which the object was probably launched, and then noted the son sitting in that chair. Raymond Sr. nodded to himself as if adding a stroke to a tally next to a son's name and continued his conversation with the other workers without a hitch.

The show seemingly over, Justin and Elizabeth headed toward the back porch. Georgette gently placed a hand on Elizabeth's shoulder, stopping the duo in their tracks. A quick instruction was whispered, to which Elizabeth returned a knowing smile. While Georgette talked to his sister, Justin's eyes tracked a plate of iced jam cake. Justin slipped his hand from Elizabeth's to follow this treasure just a step behind the plate carrier. As soon as the plate hit the table, and the plate carrier's skirts were in retreat back to the kitchen for more food, Justin's hand shot out to catch a bit of icing off the side of the plate. But his finger barely got a smidgen of the icing, thanks to Elizabeth who had chased him down. Once he was in hand, Elizabeth snatched him up into the air and ran with him shoulder high. Justin squealed all the way, delighted by the ride. They reached the back porch, Elizabeth held him head high so he could reach the bell rope. Justin quickly realized that he had been chosen as the "ringer" for this meal. Without further invitation, Justin grabbed the rope and tugged vigorously, resulting in their family's "call to the table" coded ring. A gleefully peeling rhythm of one ring then a three-second wait, followed by three short blasts, a three second wait, and a final bang on the bell. No other family within earshot would think they were being called to eat. Only the Huhn's had that ring. When the ringing was completed, Elizabeth sat him down and Justin hit the ground running. He dashed directly to the jam cake and this time succeeded in scooping a huge finger full of icing off the cake edge. He popped the favorite from his finger into his mouth, plopped his buns onto his chair, and placed folded angelic hands in front of him on the table in what seemed to be one fluid motion.

The clusters of men and klatches of women instantly took their places at the tables upon hearing the bell's call. Elizabeth pursued Justin to the table and took her seat next to him. Everyone was at the table but Doug. Raymond Sr. and Georgette glanced at one another from opposite ends of the table. A slight shrug from Georgette and Raymond Sr. continued the process.

"Let us bow our heads in prayer." The obliging guests reached out to grasp hands, forming a ring around the table. "Lucky for the guest on the other side of Justin," thought Elizabeth, "I have the side with the sticky icing fingers." She smiled to herself and thanked God for one sweet brother out of the lot. Raymond Sr.'s prayer continued on top of her own.

"Dear Heavenly Father, bless this food to nourish our bodies in order that we might put our hands to work for your purposes." A slight disturbance at the table signified to all those trying to be reverent and keep their eyes closed and their concentration on God, that Doug had just joined them. Georgette opened one eye to check out her theory.

Sure enough, he was there in his seat, head bowed, and hands clasped defiantly in front of him, making it necessary for those on either side of his seat to continue to hold hands in front of him in order to keep the circle unbroken. Georgette made a note of this detail and bowed her head and closed her eyes again to rejoin the prayer. "May we truly make ourselves deserving of your great love. In Jesus' name we pray. Amen."

In unison the women dropped their hands from the ring of prayer, sprang up from their seats, and headed for the kitchen where the food had been waiting, covered in their serving bowls, in an effort to keep the dishes hot through the prayer. The men started to pass the food already on the table. Elizabeth poured coffee, lemonade, or water as she circled the table with Justin holding a bowl of ice chips and the third pitcher for Elizabeth. The four older boys were putting scoops of food on one another's plates and giggling about it. Raymond now had a huge scoop of pickled beets on his plate, a dish he abhorred. Wishing to put them back, he tried to grab the bowl but was too late to retrieve it—the beet bowl had already rounded the next corner of the table.

Raymond Sr. sensed a need for control. His gaze rested on Raymond Jr.'s plate and a brief smirk crossed his lips. "Boys, don't forget, take what you want but eat what you take. I expect clean plates." Raymond Jr.'s lips appeared to be forming protest but he must have thought better of it. Instead Raymond Jr. forked a beet, stuffed it in his mouth, and tried to chew it. He swallowed hard to force it down. Satisfied that for once he had been heard, Raymond Sr. turned his attention back to the food on his plate. The deflected attention of his dad allowed Junior to get one beet to the ground without detection. A gift the lamb soon found and ate readily.

The women reappeared at the table with a turkey platter full of half-inch-thick slices of ham with a centered crowning bowl of red-eye gravy. Georgette, with Josey behind her duplicating her efforts, carried a platter filled with roasted half chickens, gravy boat and ladle center stage. Wendolina placed a full water pitcher of chicken gravy as an auxiliary supply on the table with one hand and a second pitcher of sausage gravy on the table with the other hand. The main course was deemed served when Georgette regained her seat.

Jeffery flicked a pea at Justin, but hit Elizabeth instead. Without a word Raymond Sr. extended a two-foot-long arm the impossible six-foot span between himself and Jeffery. The hand at the end of this six-foot arm knocked the back of Jeffery's head so hard that the whole table stopped simultaneously for one chew to appreciate the moment's impact. The faces around the table showed no emotion at all to this action except for the one Sunday school teacher whose knowing and approving smile seemed to celebrate the discipline wholeheartedly.

"These cucumbers are excellent!" Raymond Sr. proclaimed as he held up a forkful and scooped them eagerly into his mouth.

"Thank you, Father." Elizabeth beamed.

"Did you make these?"

"Yes." Elizabeth tried to be modest as the whole table sang the praises of the applauded dish or asked for them to be passed their way now that the dish had such a high rating.

"Excellent, just excellent," added Raymond Sr. "Thank you," Elizabeth offered again with a blush now that the fuss was from the whole table. Well, that was except for the three middle brothers who were mimicking the delight of the adults. Ignoring the antics of those sons, Georgette frosted Elizabeth's cake for her. "Yes, she's becoming quite a cook, and a great baby-sitter for Justin, too."

Justin was indignant. "I ain't no baby."

Georgette smiled warmly at her youngest. "Of course not. You are getting to be a big boy."

Both Georgette and Raymond Sr. glared at the four older boys who had continued to pile food on one another's plates. "You'll sit here until those plates are empty," Raymond Sr. intoned.

The men ate heartily and claimed they had no room for dessert when their plates were removed and the pies were brought out. Somehow they managed to eat one apple, two cherry, and three pumpkin pies before they stopped. The boys got no pie because they were still eating the food on their plates. Justin had passed up much of the meal in favor of the jam cake and no one stopped him from indulging.

The women retired to the kitchen to wash the dishes as the men slowly wound their way to a spot behind the barn. As the menfolk walked, they prepared a pipe full of tobacco or deftly rolled a cigarette. Once behind the barn, the silence was rarely broken as they shared that rare phenomenon that is male bonding, something that is satisfactorily completed without the spoken word. Unless the weather and crops needed to be scrutinized, there were no vocalizations except those that drifted up on a rare breeze from the romping children. A stubbed-out cigar appeared from a worn cotton pocket—a seldom seen pleasure, which was obviously giving much delight to the owner who closed his eyes as each puff was released into the air. Matches were struck on the steel toes of work boots or in some fashion specific to that individual. One hand preferred to strike the match head by pulling it across the surface of his front tooth edge in a way that never failed to startle at least someone in whatever gaggle of men he found himself.

The shade of the barn was a welcome benefit on this hot late summer day. The men waited for this, the worst heat of the day, to pass with the excuse of waiting for digestion. Like waiting to go in swimming after you eat, the myth was used to grant a much-needed restful time in a culture that allowed only disrespect for idleness. "Hands to work and hearts to God" or "Idle hands are the devil's workshop" had been heard so much in their formative years that the German work ethic prevailed to a fault. Thus, any restful pause would require some rationalization. The men, justified this reprieve from the fields for medical reasons, enjoyed their smokes in the American barnyard equivalent of the English manor's study where the men retired to brandy and cigars, leaving the womenfolk alone to sort out the gossip of the day. The equivalents in terms of a Depression-era sharecropper were "behind the barn" for the men and "doing the dishes" for the women. The rest hadn't changed much. The women gossiped and the men diplomatically looked for some safe topic or just let the silence reign. So much of the potential conversation material was taboo in polite circles.

Information traveled slowly for those without a radio, so those with one tried to share what they could without appearing to brag about the fact that they did own a radio. It would be rude to offer the latest news, so those with the magic wonder waited patiently for their friends and acquaintances to pull the information out of them instead. Some of the men sat on upturned kegs, some on stumps, and some on logs that had been rolled into the shade, while others chose to lean up against the barn, one foot perpendicular to the wall. The smoke rose and drifted quickly off on the warm breezes. The pipers made rings that were twisted and distorted before they reached eye level.

"So, George, that new radio of yours, got anything worth sharing on it lately?" Raymond Sr. as host was expected to break the customary silence first. He was always eager to learn about the world beyond his forty-acre view.

"Well," George replied ever so slowly, as if pulling some thoughts out of the woods and dragging them to the tree line for further transportation, "seems the war in Europe is still leaning in favor of Germany. But the English have dug in and won't give up. Churchill is directly pleading with FDR to help out. Time will tell where we go from here."

The kitchen talk wasn't much different. Politeness required that most topics be avoided. The mention of the childbirthing difficulties of one member would be met with a worried gaze at Elizabeth and that topic would quickly be abandoned to prevent any questions from the youngest dish drier to the hostess dishwasher later in the evening. The offending conversationalist would blush and move on to a more neutral topic or be saved by another drier and all the adults would move the changed topic along. News of members of the community was monitored so that it would stay on the level of deep Christian concern and helpfulness. The minute the tone changed to one of potential judgment, an eyebrow would lift somewhere in the group and a more constructive angle was soon developed into the stream, and thus by example "gossip" or "inappropriate talk" was halted. So many topics of great interest to Elizabeth—like how babies were born, how babies got there in the first place, and who was this aunt they all seemed to complain about—rarely received the in-depth coverage that would help Elizabeth sort it all out.

It seemed like such a coincidence that all these women would have a common relative. How could all of them share this one relative, which they all complained about in unison? Yet, much to Elizabeth's frustration, none of these topics ever reached a level of total explanation.

After a while, Elizabeth's kitchen duties were deemed "helpful enough" and she was released to go play with Justin. However, the minute she left the room, the conversation picked up to a lively pace. As Elizabeth exited the kitchen through the living room, she paused to listen just a bit to confirm her suspicions. Yes, the topics she longed to have answers to were now being discussed. Elizabeth was sure that there were some membership dues that allowed one to join this inner circle, dues she had not yet paid. Try as she would to eavesdrop on the new conversational energy, she could hear but fragments. Justin wouldn't stop chattering long enough for Elizabeth to weave a coherent thought together from the conversational scraps she could collect from the kitchen. Eventually she tired of the challenge and she and Justin went outside to hunt bullfrogs in an attempt to escape the heat of the house in the afternoon sun.

"Maybe we'll catch some big enough to eat." Justin's eyes glistened with the thought of the taste of the water-flavored meat of frog's legs, breaded and fried in his mom's big cast-iron skillet.

"Yeah, frog legs." Elizabeth's gaze reflected Justin's enthusiasm.

"Let's try Wilker's pond." Justin dashed off down the drive with Elizabeth close behind.

Georgette, ever vigilant, saw the exodus of two of her flock and ran to the back door. "Where are you two going?"

Elizabeth turned around to run backward to shout her reply, "Wilker's pond—catch frogs."

Georgette shook her head and turned back to the kitchen still gently smiling and rotating her head from side to side.

"Where they headed?"

"Don't really know. Catchin' frogs is all I got of it. But Elizabeth has a lot of sense—so it'll be somewhere close." Georgette admitted that often she asked her children where they were going just to let them know she cared about them and that she was watching. The answers weren't that necessary.

"Wilker's pond or Seakin's creek?" a helper volunteered.

"Exactly," Georgette put away the last pan, wiped her hands on her apron, gave a final look around the kitchen, and nodded an approval. With that, the ladies retired to the afternoon shade of the porch. The first time they'd sat down, except to eat, since 5 A.M.

"OK, let's rest a spell before we fix 'em dinner." The ladies each reached for a piece of needlework, which rested in the ladies' aproned laps as they chatted, worked the stitching, and sipped iced tea. Pure idleness was never really an option.

By now the men had wandered from the shade of the barn's shadow and had started working the fields again. They would work until sunset. Then they would snack on the sandwiches that the ladies would have put out for them made from the lunch leftovers. After the informal supper, both men and women would drop into their beds like stones. The next day they would roll out of bed and do it all over again at another neighbor's farm until every farmer's crops in this small co-op were in. The exhaustion factor was a big reason that harvest was such a big celebration. It meant recess was finally in order after months of backbreaking work.

The Huhn farm harvesting activity shot a plume of dust into the air. Thanks to the thrashing machine, the seven-man team could bring in a day's worth of crops in what would have taken seven days by hand. It made it well worth

the men's while to rent the machine from the grain elevator. The rental fee would be deducted from the payment on
the grain.

The whole community could be spied on by casting a
gaze over the horizon. There would be plumes reporting
where the thrashing machines were working throughout the
county. The ladies watched the activity from their porch
seats and discussed who else was harvesting that day that
they might know. At the same time their needlepoint was
worked about as fast as their mouths. They glanced up to
make sure that the reassuring plume was still coming from
the field where their men worked.

Georgette's hands flew as she tatted, a skill that only she
knew that well in this circle of friends. The glances that
frequently went toward her hands spoke of a subtle envy
the others felt for her unique craft. The results of her surgi-
cally precise moves were the tiniest pieces of lace-like
flowers. Little shuttles guided floss through a torturous path
with the resultant half-inch-thick icing of lace that graced
her collars and sleeves and pillowcases and table runners
and doilies. The house and Elizabeth's and Georgette's
wardrobes attested to the prolific nature of her "idle time."
Georgette's and Elizabeth's garments may have been made
of donated fabric from some hand-me-down dresses or old
curtains from some relative or church member, but Georgette would make them special with her tatting and turn
them into works of art that both girl and mom could be
proud to wear. Georgette's glance rarely was required on
the production at hand, so her gaze hunted the hedgerows
for a glimpse of Justin and Elizabeth. The two would come

home victoriously, leaping through the tall weeds if they had been successful in catching a frog, or walk slowly, dragging sticks behind them, if their hunt was futile. So far she saw no signs of these two.

The other four children were better off unheard from and so Georgette usually only became concerned if those four showed up before a meal was scheduled to be served. They wouldn't show up too soon for fear they'd be asked to help in the preparations, yet neither too late for fear that their dad would refuse them the meal to teach them to show up on time for family meals. This was a way to respect their mom's food preparation energies. Showing up before the meal was planned could only mean that one of them was hurt or that they wanted to keep some poor unfortunate creature that they had managed to wear down enough to capture. Raymond Jr. was almost old enough to help in the fields, yet he was much more help on a day like today keeping his little brothers in line.

All was right with her world and Georgette knew it. The children were healthy. The pantry had food. The crop was good and would be enough to pay the annual rent bill, which wasn't due until the crop sold. A vegetable garden had produced forty-eight jars of pickles, more of tomatoes, and twice as many of fruit for winter pies. In fact, she'd run out of jars to can the bounty that the earth had provided. Maybe they'd have enough cash to buy a case or two more of the good Mason jars, and buy Elizabeth a new pair of shoes and maybe even a bike for the boys for Christmas. (A used bike, but to the boys it wouldn't matter.) She reminded herself that there were so many needs on the farm that a toy hardly seemed necessary. But she'd try to talk to Raymond Sr. into it somehow...

That's when she noticed it. Her gaze had once again turned to the field and rested at the place in the sky were the thrashing dust plume had been. Her hands stopped moving, such a rare change that it caught the attention of the other porch sitters. They followed her gaze as Georgette stood up—dumping her handwork onto the porch floor-boards. The other women rose and looked in vain for the plume that should have been in the field with their men if all was still going well. Another plume was racing toward the house. A plume of dust was being sent skyward by a pickup truck going full speed.

The women rushed to fulfill Georgette's instinctively hurried orders. "Someone chop some ice. Someone else strip bandages. There's an old sheet under the stairwell. Someone is hurt. Someone's down." The last phrase she moaned as if to herself alone, a prayer of deep dread and foreboding. Mourning for one of the women and selfishly wishing for it not to be her burden to bear, yet knowing that very same thought was racing through every female mind in the house. These words had stuck in her throat. Words she'd heard before but had hoped she'd never need to utter. The needlework was utterly abandoned as she and her flock went into a flurry of Florence Nightingale preparations. Disaster was headed directly toward them. One of them had a hurt man to care for. Each of them looked at the truck in horrid anticipation that it would be their man laid out in the bed of the truck already near death from loss of blood. The nearest hospital was in Tiffin, which was another thirty minutes away.

There was a change in the horizon and Elizabeth noted the change. There wasn't any thrashing plume coming from their fields anymore. Instead there was a smaller trail of dust stirred up by a truck headed toward their house going way too fast for it not to be trouble of some kind. Justin followed her line of sight.

"What, Betsy? What's goin' on?"

"Nothin's goin' on. Let's go see if this crick has any crawdads in it." Instinctively he read her face and knew that something was wrong no matter what his sister's words were. The rest was told by the set of her jaw, which said that there was serious business here. A jaw setting that his mom also had. Heredity can't be made impotent with words. Justin knew that something bad was happening, something too bad for him to go home. He would trust his big sister and just go with her to look for the crawdads.

Elizabeth didn't want Justin to see the blood. He didn't need that any more than she did. Worse yet, he was too young to be seeing somebody die from blood loss right before his eyes. But then so was she, too young for such a picture to be permanently emblazoned on her mind's eye. So she kept him away and thus kept herself away, too. But the smile had left both their faces. Justin wondered what was going through his sister's more knowing mind, and Elizabeth prayed that it wasn't her brothers or her father. Hoping desperately that she was overreacting to the dust-plume message and nothing at all was really happening, maybe just sunstroke, or snakebite. But the truth of a har-

vest day accident was usually loss of life or limb and sometimes both.

She helped Justin over rocks to look for the paranoid
crustaceans. They'd tip over a rock and uncover a choice
specimen, but once the shadow of a potentially capturing
hand was detected by the critter it would backward scamper
under the next rock. It kept Justin busy during those moments Elizabeth needed to look homeward again. She
searched for any information that would reassure her that
brothers and father were fine, but so far her lookout position had provided no new data. It wasn't until the truck left
the driveway again at full speed, turning at the end of the
driveway toward Tiffin and thus the hospital, that she
coaxed Justin to go home. She had to know.

Elizabeth ran as fast as she could while dragging Justin
behind her. As she approached the house she could see the
ladies, some of them on their hands and knees scrubbing
the porch floor. Closer and she could see as they looked up
to acknowledge that she and Justin were coming home, the
dread and pity already in their faces. Some women acceler-
ated their pace and worked even harder at scrubbing what
looked like blood from the porch floorboards, while two of
the women approached the two children.

Elizabeth studied their eyes. She didn't like what she
saw there. Panic began to rise in her throat so that she could
only utter one word. "Mother, Mother." She began to shout
it as she opened the back porch screen door, flying over the
area being scrubbed. She even let the door bang shut just as
if she were one of her younger brothers playing tag.

Georgette was seated at the kitchen table reading her Bible. She looked up to greet her daughter's eyes. "What, Elizabeth? What do you need?"

"Tell me Father's OK. Just tell me Father's OK."

"He's in God's care—He couldn't be better...but he's hurt."

"No. No," Elizabeth moaned softly to herself.

"Yes, Elizabeth. He is hurt. He's on his way to the hospital. God willing, he'll be just fine."

"What happened?"

"The thrasher caught his hand."

"No...his hand?" Elizabeth gasped, breathless. Her eyes reflected some understanding of such a tragic event. A farmer who lost a hand rarely became successful again after such an injury.

"His whole hand?" The questions were coming at a slower pace now that the worst fears were somewhat set aside.

"No, we think just a couple of fingers."

"Oh, poor father."

"Pray with me."

Elizabeth sat next to her mother. "Anything I can do to help?" she asked with tears running down her cheeks.

"You are doing it already, dear." Georgette reached over to hold Elizabeth's hands as they bowed their heads and prayed together. The other women entered the kitchen and joined the prayer vigil without words. They bowed their heads and folded their hands. One of the women cuddled

Justin who was almost asleep in her arms already. Georgette lead them in an audible prayer ending with…

"…And may a peace that passeth all understanding enter us as we struggle to accept and work through this new trial of life. In Jesus' name we pray. Amen."

"Amen" echoed around the table and Georgette began a hymn at the chorus. The others joined in.

"Leaning, leaning, leaning on the everlasting arms. Leaning, leaning, leaning on the everlasting arms of Christ."

Justin slept and the singing continued until the truck returned.

Chapter 3

The Long Road Home

Dear Star,

I rocked Justin last night. I am so worried about my dad. What will become of us? The truck came back from the hospital with him very late. Hours of waiting and praying and secretly crying. My mom never shed a tear the whole time. She sat in the kitchen with her Bible in her lap surrounded by the other ladies who prayed, sang, and read their Bibles out loud at intervals to fill the time.

I loved the hymn singing. That is the best way to pass worry time as far as I can see. I haven't seen Dad yet. Mom says that he is in a lot of pain and is best left alone to sleep for a few days. Allow the healing to start. But the look in her eyes is not reassuring. I just wonder how bad things really are.

Wish that I were old enough to help somehow. The harvest still sits in the fields. All the time the men spent getting Dad to the hospital and medically attended to was lost from the harvest effort which had been slowed miserably. A few men did stay back to work the fields but a productive effort requires a full seven-man crew. With only four men plus Raymond Jr. who tried to help, they only got a few more acres done after the accident.

Pray for us, dear Star.

Elizabeth

By the time the truck came back, Justin and the boys had been put to bed. Elizabeth tried to wait up with the women but fell asleep on the living room couch. By now the whole community, well at least those with telephones, had spread the news. Physicians' wives, nurses, and their families all knew that Raymond Huhn Sr. had lost all four fingers on his left hand before anyone in the Huhn household had heard a word. The Huhn farm and ninety percent of the farms had no phone. A call had gone to Raymond Sr.'s father, Burkhardt Huhn, and Raymond's stepmother—a call of consideration from someone who assumed that Raymond Sr.'s family would want to know and help.

"Hello," Raymond Sr.'s stepmother, Patiens, had remembered to answer the phone in English for a change instead of her native tongue, German. But regardless of the language she chose, even the "Hello" was sweetly spoken.

After listening for a few brief moments, Patiens handed the phone to Burkhardt as he entered the kitchen. He grabbed the phone from Patiens and began speaking rudely into the phone.

"Yes, this is the house of Raymond Sr.'s parents. What's he done now? Gone and had another kid? Another mouth to feed when he can't even feed the one's he's got?" Burkhardt anticipated in his usual condescending tone. His face softened ever so slightly then dug even deeper ridges into his forehead as he took in the news from the other end of the phone.

"Oh, so someone probably thinks that we should get involved. Well, we have enough debts of our own without adding every ne'er-do-well relative onto our own personal dole list." Burkhardt listened a few seconds to the caller and gave his final reply, his jowls so animated that they slapped into his Adam's apple as he jabbed his pointed finger into the chest of the wall next to the phone.

"Auf wiedersehen. Sure, I'll tell her." The phone receiver returned to its resting place next to the double brass bells of the magneto-wood wall phone with enough energy to cause Patiens to jump a bit from her breakfast table chair.

The call ended, Burkhardt stood in the doorway, shaking his head and smiling a fiend's smile with a deeply furrowed brow.

"Everything OK?" Patiens asked as she offered her moon-round face another piece of bacon.

"Yah, just Raymond Sr. Seems he lost part of his hand in a thrashing accident today. The whole community thinks now that this is our problem."

Burkhardt took his seat across the table from his plump second wife.

"Goodness, you had me worried. Usually you only talk to the revenuers that way. What are we going to do?" Patiens nodded to herself. Burkhardt turned his attention to the farm reports on the kitchen radio with a more relaxed look on his face. No more was said about Raymond Sr. or his hand by either man or wife throughout the remainder of their morning meal. Burkhardt sipped black strong coffee while his dear mound of a wife finished a plate of pancakes and sausage.

By the time the returning truck's headlights started up the Huhn farm driveway, some of the women with Georgette had been periodically checking the mantel clock and wondering how much longer it would be until the truck returned. Each minute meant that the injury was worse than they had thought. To stay busy, they had made coffee and arranged some desserts on the table for the men when they came in. The men just might be hungry. It had been a long time since the noon meal. Many of the women sipped coffee and nibbled the cakes or pies. Some women had started snapping peas for the next day's meal. The Huhn family would need all the help they could get for a while. The boys were small for their ages and no way near capable of farming without adult supervision. Georgette, Raymond Jr., and Elizabeth could do some things around the farm but the community would have to supply the pieces that Raymond

Sr. couldn't do. Many farms were barely making ends meet with every hand busy eighteen hours a day. How would anyone be able to spare the hours needed for someone else's farm? These unspoken worries filled their minutes of waiting.

Aunt Emily and Uncle Howard eventually received a call from Burkhardt telling Howard of his half brother's misfortune. The childless couple stayed up talking half the night. Talking about the ramifications of the unfortunate event and what they could do to help. Six children to one brother who could barely afford one and no children to the real estate broker brother who could afford a dozen or more and clothe them like royalty and send them to college. Each life has its tests to pass or fail. The current test, in Emily's words, "would be a test of faith for both brothers."

The Ladies' Auxiliary chairwoman, Emma-Lou Snodgrass and her sister cochair, Ida, were of course notified of the accident by the hospital chaplain, a cousin. Since the sisters had received the news, they had been calling other church members and plotting the best way to assist. But mostly they debated between the two of them the best rescue plan.

Emma-Lou was a proponent of doing as little as possible to be sure that the needy didn't become "lazy," as she called it. Nor did she want the community's generosity to transform the family into a long-term dependent. Ida's position was much more generous. Ida was willing to risk dependence so that she could rest better knowing the needy were comfortable. Emma-Lou's position was a precursor to the Mother Theresa approach while Ida's was more an "ask and you shall receive" philosophy. Who's to really know which is truly "Heaven's Gate"? Maybe neither. Maybe either. Who's to know for sure if deeds open or close the Pearly Gates at all?

The set of lights coming up the driveway woke Elizabeth as they flashed through each successive window. The women peered from the kitchen windows. Georgette sat at the table, hands folded.

"I don't want to look too worried. It may be best for him to see me looking strong and silent," she had whispered to a close friend. The door opened and two men, two husbands of the attending ladies, came in. One wife questioned, "So where is Raymond Sr.?" looking at Georgette as she said it as if to say, "I'll say it for you." Georgette nodded a small "thank you" for the question.

"Right behind us in a second truck," he replied and patted his wife's hand. His heavy boots rang out on the wood floor. This was the only sound in the kitchen as he walked over and sat next to Georgette.

"I hate to be the one to have to tell you this, but we thought it would be best for you to know before he got here."

"Thank you, I appreciate the gesture." She reached out and patted his hand. "It's OK. You can tell me. I'm prepared."

"Georgette, they saved the rest of his hand…" He finished telling her about the hospital's efforts until the second truck's lights could be seen flashing through the rows of unharvested corn as the truck rumbled down the country road toward the driveway. The lights turned into the drive as Georgette asked her only question.

"How is he taking this?"

"He's in a lot of pain. He seems overwhelmed by it all—dazed." The husband paused. "But surely he'll be OK in a few days."

Georgette's forehead furrowed slightly as she took in the report. Physical disabilities were difficult to overcome with a positive attitude. What about his outlook? His attitude could make a big difference in his ability to cope. She'd wait and watch and pray and work for two. That was all a good Christian wife could do.

There was no "love gift" on her pillow that night. It was God who bestowed the "love gift" to Georgette that night. Raymond Sr. had survived and lay there on the pillow next to hers. This was a "love gift" enough for that day's end.

Chapter 4

The Pains of Religion

Dear Star,

Good news at church on Sunday. Some men volunteered to help us get the rest of our crops in. Our neighbors also needed help since the team was down one hand. Raymond Jr. tried to help again but his inexperience led to him being delegated to truck driver.

Bad news. My feet haven't shrunk since my last trip to church.

Dad and Mom still look worried all the time. They go off in other rooms to talk a lot. They always discuss farm issues out of earshot is my guess. That's how they always talked business, away from the kids. But there seems to be a lot more of these now than in the past.

I must have inherited Mom's worrywart gene.

Wishing on you, my personal Star, that all will go well.

Justin pointed out his favorite star to me last night. I wished on it, too. Mostly that I would never get growths on my chest like my mom's cousin had! Didn't look like a good thing to have happen to you. Totally filled her lap when she sat down.

Good night for now.

Elizabeth

Giving idle hands usefulness may be one reason God plants so many tragedies in our field of dreams, which is life. Someone must be needy to test another's will to give. The news of the Huhn family tragedy brought out the best in some, the worst in others.

The Ladies' Auxiliary had already decided their game plan. The men in the church would take care of the crops while the womenfolk would take care of the family. First an envoy of two—Emma-Lou and Ida, of course—would visit the family to assess the current situation. But Emma-Lou won her way. This was almost their favorite part of helping someone: the spy mission. How do they live? What clothing needs do they have? What standards need to be maintained, "at a minimum level," Emma-Lou would constantly remind. Spoiling the recipients into a pattern of need was not an honorable path. Ida disagreed. Ida just loved to give. And, she had a lot to give. Emma usually got her way during the debate, Ida would slip a few extras into the care packages at just the last second, and Emma-Lou would admit it was too late to argue the point anymore. Ida pulled this off while they were on the porch. Ida had learned to hide boxed chocolates and even an extra chicken under her coat, totally undetected by Emma-Lou. Emma was beginning to consider frisking Ida before they left the church on these missions. But that would just be too embarrassing for both of them and Emma-Lou had decided to let the game continue, finding no good way to stop it.

Their first spying session was easy. The whole Huhn family came to church the Sunday after the accident. Obviously the family was relying on God's strength to pull them through the tough times ahead. That got big points from the sisters.

The Huhn brood approached the church door in a ragtaggle stop-and-start burst-and-collapse pattern of energy which took its pulse from the four younger boys in the back, then the front, and then the back again of the family procession, each one of them barefoot. Yelping would be sent out of one young mouth as he stubbed his toe on the uneven sidewalk. A younger brother was attempting to elude capture by another brother. Once recovered from the pain, the assaulted boy ran past his assailant and snapped a suspender so hard it echoed against the church walls. With a tear in his eye, the snappee began a new round of retaliation. Order was restored by a mere tilt of Raymond Sr.'s head in the direction of the children behind him. That was suggestion enough for Elizabeth and Raymond Jr. to turn to their little brothers and shake a scolding finger at them. Or, if a brother were close enough, Elizabeth would grab an arm and force-march them next to her. Raymond Jr.'s technique was to try to trip them. Once on the ground he would grab them by the waistband and drag them along beside him with their head locked under his elbow. Elizabeth would give Raymond Jr. a reproachful look, which only received a shrug and eventual release of a more subdued brother. "Hey, whatever works!" was Raymond Jr.'s only comment.

Raymond Jr. was the only son to have shoes. Elizabeth winced at almost every step as she tried curling her toes away from the front of her shoes. These shoes were hand-me-downs as well as the dress material that her mother had refashioned into something that fit. But the shoes were pure torture. She was a teenager now and this pair of shoes made her look nine years old. She was the offspring of two very short people. Needless to say, she had those genes. A slight stature just made it all the more difficult to grow up. Everyone still wanted to treat her like a little kid.

Elizabeth had argued with her mother, begging to go barefoot instead of wearing those shoes again. Georgette, however, did not think it proper for a girl of thirteen to go to church barefoot. The torture of the shoes was a far better choice. "Besides, life is full of pain. It builds character," had been the last argument about the shoes allowed. Georgette got a certain look in her eyes when a topic had been closed for discussion. All her flock knew that look and respected it. Elizabeth had already formulated next Sunday's argument. "A girl of thirteen should be in heels. Let me wear a pair of your shoes, mother." She'd worked on this one all week, playing it back and forth in her head and in front of the mirror, until she got it just right.

"Proper schmopper," came out of Elizabeth's mouth just under her breath. Startled at the sound of her own voice, she looked up to see that Georgette's pallor was painted with an even more vicious-looking stare. Bowing her head in submission and locking her lips shut tight, Elizabeth shrunk away to her room to retrieve the offensive shoes.

Hand-me-downs were easy for the boys, from Senior to Junior to the little boys. While it didn't always look so great by the time Justin got it, Justin seemed to like the patched knees and elbows.

For Elizabeth the hand-me-downs were different. More than once a discard would come to Elizabeth that would be remade for years, as she grew into and out of the various options available—dresses redesigned into blouses, for example. Once her mother's cousin, who weighed the same as a prize sow at the county fair, brought a whole bag of clothes for Georgette to "rework." Upon her leaving, they discovered that the bag only contained two dresses.

During the visit Elizabeth was quite subdued. She was preoccupied with sadness for this second cousin, for as well as Elizabeth could figure, she didn't have long to live given her condition. Georgette asked after the cousin had left, "Elizabeth, why so quiet? Are you feeling all right?"

"Yes, mother, I feel just fine. But she had those growths on her chest. Will she die soon?"

"What growths?"

"Those big saggy things."

Georgette started to laugh, then quickly stifled it to explain, "Those are breasts, Elizabeth, like a cow's udders, for milk, for babies." Georgette saw a light go off behind the eyes and knew her daughter had just had an epiphany.

Elizabeth looked at her mother's flat chest and then down to her own. Georgette responded, "The Lord grants everyone some gifts but not all of them to everyone." Elizabeth paused to consider this, another bit of sage wisdom from her mother.

"So having big ones is a gift?"

"Some people think so." Georgette went on examining the contents of the bag. Her attention was now on the bag of tent dresses that she would transform into stylish clothing for Elizabeth and herself. The patterns were a bit disappointing but wondered what a little of her lace could do to distract the eye.

As the Huhn family walked up the steps of the church, the observant person would notice that the same fabric that was worn by Elizabeth and Georgette would also be worn by the two youngest brothers who would have shirts made out of the same old dress. Back home there were curtains in the pantry that also matched. Thank goodness for large relatives.

The pastor, who was the perfect rendition of an old German beet farmer, waited just inside the church door to greet each family as they entered. As the Huhn family approached, Raymond Sr. and Georgette paid their respects while their tribe went to pieces behind them. Winston was playing monkey in the middle with Elizabeth's shoulder purse, using Jeffery and Doug as coconspirators. As the purse was tossed once more over Doug's head, it snapped open and rained out the contents all over the waiting arms of Jeffery. Raymond Jr. stood laughing as Elizabeth scrambled to pick up her valuables. Tears streamed down her face as she collected a now broken face mirror and a tiny lipstick sample that Georgette did not know that Elizabeth owned. Elizabeth picked up the now soiled handkerchief and dabbed at a tear track on her cheek. The small change that Elizabeth had brought for the collection rolled into sidewalk cracks and her brothers quickly sought out the coins and placed them in their own pockets. A look from Raymond Sr. and a step in their direction sent all five boys into military attention while Elizabeth finished putting herself back together. Wiping her other cheek with the back of her hand and her nose with her finger sent a shudder of realization through Elizabeth and her dirty hanky came back out of her purse to dab her nose instead. Georgette watched her daughter make the substitution and Georgette proudly smiled as she entered the church. One of her brood was indeed going to turn out civilized.

Raymond Sr. turned to the boys and with his back to the preacher, put his hand on his belt buckle as if to unleash it to demonstrate to his offspring that he would be willing to remove his belt and could with only one good hand if he had to. Looks of disbelief and renewed respect glimmered on the faces of the boys, demonstrating that Raymond Sr.'s message had been delivered and understood.

Small clumps of adults bundled outside on the church sidewalk, visiting and enjoying the bright sun of an early October day. Emma-Lou and Ida were clucking away in their gaggle of friends that made up the Ladies' Auxiliary. Emma-Lou sneered at the antics of the Huhn boys and turned the attention of her group to that display of youthful energy.

"It's simply shameful that those boys aren't disciplined."

"Oh, sister," Ida defended, "I know for certain that he doesn't spare the rod. It just does no good."

"Heathens," Emma-Lou seethed in retort. "They don't even wear shoes to church."

Ida, knowing that it was useless to argue further, replied mostly to herself, "Perhaps they don't have any." Emma heard something but didn't really know what and was always keen to continue the debate. Emma tried to keep Ida involved. "What was that?"

Ida reflected on the need to take action to help rather than to be content to pass judgment. "Oh, nothing…just thinking that maybe we should pay them that visit to see what they might need."

Taking action and getting involved in fixing other people's lives so that their lives more nearly conformed to her standards was Ida's favorite activity. This activity kept her life interesting and busy. There are only so many bandages you could roll in a lifetime. She and the Ladies' Auxiliary group had rolled bandages for the Great War until they needed a few of those bandages for their own sore fingers. But, because of their contribution, victory had also been won. They had helped fight the good fight from a small Ohio town with bandages that may have wrapped the wounds of one of their town's boys who had volunteered to fight for freedom in a European war.

Then the Depression had rolled its dark cloud over the world. The Ladies' Auxiliary had seen some of its own members sink to a financial low that had frightened the moneyed folks in church to vow to help their own first. Who knew whose fortune would be secure and whose would evaporate next? Best to be sympathetic to the situation of the poor and try not to judge them guilty of some trespass for which they deserved their ruin. Then if it happened to them, others would hopefully also be sympathetic.

So Emma-Lou and Ida helped as much as they could in the community. They steered out-of-work husbands to the WPA work sites across the region. Often they gave the bus fare for such journeys out of their own purse rather than bother with the red tape of getting the Ladies' Auxiliary involved. That way fewer folks in the church would know the plight of that particular family. The unpublished charity would hopefully lessen the gossip and save some pride for a fellow church member and his family. Few people in the community knew of these generous, anonymous deeds. With hearts in the right place, Emma-Lou and Ida could still make a mess of it, though. Humble yet annoying, they would usually cause some troubles because of their lack of tact and diplomacy. Well meaning but poorly spoken is often less beneficial than poorly done but well said.

"You're right!" Emma finally agreed. "Even though Raymond Sr.'s father is filthy rich from his black market deals, that doesn't mean the father is sharing any of it with his son. Raymond Sr. hasn't been able to work for weeks now. With Thanksgiving coming, we could put them on the Ladies' Auxiliary list for a Thanksgiving food basket." Emma Lou was in high gear now.

"Good idea. I bet his father hasn't helped at all," Ida added.

"Shameful greedy man." One of the other ladies finally managed to get a word in between the sisters' bantering.

"Word has it that his second wife is pure as driven snow. Why would she have chosen such a man?" Emma Lou had found a bone to chew on now and she was going to keep at this topic until some shame could be forced out of a man who wasn't even present.

Ida shook her head vigorously in agreement. "Such an angry man. Word has it he chose her particularly for her size. He made a trip back to Germany to find himself a pure German-bred wife. She was a very plump, slight-of-stature schoolteacher who wanted to immigrate to America badly enough to marry him. Apparently they each have what they want."

"A viper of a man," another lady added.

"Nothing at all like the son. One of the farmers that was helping in the field on the day of the accident said that Raymond Sr. had gotten into the truck and was going to drive himself to the hospital. None of the other men noticed what had happened until they were curious as to why Raymond Sr. had dropped everything and had run to the truck."

"So glad that they stopped him from driving himself," Emma added.

"Yes, the bandages that the ladies put on him before they drove him to the hospital probably saved his life."

"Yep, the doctors said he'd have died of blood loss without the first aid that he received.

"Too bad they can't just sew fingers back on."

"Don't be crazy!" Emma chided the silly lady who had offered such a preposterous idea.

The church bells struck a three-fold amen, signifying some message understood by all those sidewalk gossipers who now bowed their heads and funneled piously into the church like someone pulled the bathtub plug and the water rolled effortlessly down the drain and out of sight.

Elizabeth waited with her family to obtain a seat in the back pew, hopefully a back seat so that the head thumping that was required to keep these troops in line would be witnessed by no more fellow worshipers than necessary. Georgette disliked public displays of affection and discipline. She winced every time Raymond Sr. grabbed a boy's elbow and whispered in an offender's ear until the ear was reddened by the sheer heat of his angry breath. Elizabeth held Justin's hand while dancing from one foot to another. This shuffling caught Justin's attention.

"What's wrong, 'Lizbeth?"

A tear in her eye, she replied, "I'd rather be barefoot than wear these shoes, but Mom..." Elizabeth stopped herself. There was no way Justin would understand the parent-teenager battles for independence that were waging in her mind. He didn't need to hear any of that. So Elizabeth just pointed to her shoes and finished, "These are way too small, Justin."

Justin squeezed her hand in sympathy as they reached a back pew. Once seated, Elizabeth popped off the shoes. Georgette looked down the pew at her daughter in hopes of getting eye contact. Elizabeth watched via her peripheral vision as her mother leaned over and looked in Elizabeth's direction. Elizabeth was trying not to acknowledge her mother's stare, even though she could see that her mother was trying to communicate with someone down the pew. Elizabeth tactfully refused eye contact as a way to prevent a feeling of a need to comply with her mother's wishes.

Georgette was too far down the pew to say anything about the shoes or lack thereof. The four older brothers finally had some use, as they were the barriers between Elizabeth and her mother. No greater communications chasm could be built. Even if Georgette attempted to send a message down the row of sons to her daughter, the content of her intended words would probably not reach Elizabeth's ears. Georgette knew that she had little hope of getting any meaningful communication through those lines. Georgette finally rested back in her seat, uneasy, hoping no one could see her daughter's bare feet, and tried to concentrate on the service instead.

Rarely would Elizabeth disobey or do anything to displease her mother, but today, over the shoes, she needed to assert a bit of teenage independence. Everyone draws a line somewhere, sometime, and for Elizabeth it made no sense to sustain great physical pain just to avoid the worry of "What will people think?" Quite frankly, she didn't care if anyone thought they were poor or not because everyone knew that they were poor. What was the issue? Pride, of course. Was this the pride before the fall? Or had the Huhn family already hit bottom? Can't fall when you're already on the bottom, now, can you?

The twig season had arrived again. Lonesome branches pleaded with the cruel wind to return their beautiful garments of orange and red and gold that lay brown, indecipherable among the other browns sharing Mother Nature's floor. Sculpted black snakes traveled parallel paths down the fields now turned to rest. Dirt so dark it could have been the coalfields of West Virginia if only the land weren't so flat. Heck, a good sledding hill could be a half-hour's walk away. Elizabeth filled her head with thoughts such as these rather than pay attention to the sermon. They could make her go to church but they couldn't make her listen. God was letting too many bad things happen to her family. Just maybe he wasn't a loving, forgiving Father after all. Maybe she had done something to cause Him to be displeased. She couldn't bear the thought that she might be responsible for her father's injury. Best not to listen to the sermons right now for fear a finger would be pointed directly at her.

Chapter 5

The Response

Dear Star,

Raymond Jr. was talking about driving a car in a few years. Dad said he could drive now at fourteen years of age as long as it was doing farm work or maybe taking us kids to school in the snow if it got really bad. Mom doesn't drive. Never has, never will, I guess, so Raymond Jr. being able to run farm errands if Dad can't, would be a great help.

Too bad we don't have a car for him. I think that Raymond would really like to have something grown-up to tinker with instead of hanging out with his pesky little brothers.

I spoke up about driving someday and Dad said that that wouldn't happen. He said women shouldn't drive. He said that most accidents were caused by women being allowed on the road.

Mom saw my disappointment. She reached out and patted me on the leg to keep me from arguing back. Arguing with Dad is not allowed. Yet sometimes I just want to yell my opinion back at them both at the top of my lungs. Something has saved me so far every time. I'm sure the retribution (just learned that one in school) would not be worth it. I can always keep my hopes for my grown-up life to myself for now.

Elizabeth

A 1939 Ford sedan, traveling quickly toward the Huhn farm, interrupted the desolate quiet of late autumn. Black car against the black fields meant that the only indicator of its presence was its motion. The vehicle pointed straight down the road with a fair amount of jostling through the potholes and ruts. The Ford's destination could be the Huhn family farm, yet it traveled a mite too fast if the driver was serious about entering their driveway.

Ida was all dressed in her Sunday-best hat with the veil over her eyes. Emma Lou was at her sister's side, similarly dressed but her veil was pulled up. Emma's eyes darted nervously about from road to the driver, to the quickly approaching farm and its driveway entrance. Emma Lou's gaze fixated on a pothole ahead and she raised her arms as if to grab the wheel, paused with indecision, then grabbed the wheel and shouted at the driver simultaneously.

"Miss it!" Emma Lou was shaken so hard as they hit the pothole that her veil popped down off her hat. She struggled with the veil so she could see again. With a few tugs, Emma did manage to get the veil pushed up again. Getting the road back in view didn't necessarily improve the situation.

Ida angrily reacted. "Don't ever grab the wheel like that, Emma Lou."

"Well, learn to drive and miss those dern potholes. Now look what you've done. Made me curse!" Emma Lou said, still aggravated.

"Watch your tongue!" Ida replied. "You of all people have no business telling me how to drive. You can't even get a driver's license."

"That policeman wouldn't know a good driver if he was hit by one." Emma Lou fussed with her ruffles, which were snagging on her locket necklace.

"My point exactly," Ida chimed back. "Running over his foot during the driver's test hardly earns you of a license."

Another pothole jolted them. This time the Sunday-best hat that Ida wore slipped below her eye level. Ida let go of the wheel to fix her hat and Emma Lou grabbed the wheel again, trying desperately to keep the car on the road. Emma Lou's recommended style was to swerve from one side of the road to the other to miss every imperfection on the road's surface. Ida finished putting her hat back together and took her attention from her own reflection in the rear-view mirror to the fact that Emma had the wheel again. Ida took the wheel from Emma Lou with vigor and glared at her while she gave one offending hand a slap. The slap was with enough force to convince Emma that Ida was serious about this wheel-grabbing offense. The blow was enough to get Emma to relinquish control of the wheel back to Ida. Their spat ended, Ida looked ahead to realize that they were but a few feet from the Huhn family driveway. On these icy roads, a skilled driver would have found it prudent to go on past the Huhn driveway, turn around, and make a new approach. But Ida was not a prudent driver; she stomped on the brakes and headed sideways down the county road.

The black Ford sedan came to a stop with the front of the car pointed straight into the driveway. Ida recovered from the dishevelment of the slide to notice that the car was in perfect position to enter the driveway. Ida gave a know-it-all look of pride to Emma in response to Emma's irritated but silent scowl. Ida hit the gas and they jolted down the Huhn driveway. Emma glared at Ida.

"Don't you say a thing," Ida threatened in response to the look.

Emma pointed wordlessly to herself and shrugged mockingly.

Ida drove the issue and the car to their destination with a sharp brake. The car stopped at the end of a dirt path that led to the back porch and kitchen door. "I still haven't run over anyone!"

"Yet." Emma added her one-word finale under her breath as she exited the car.

"What did you say?"

"Nothing—really."

"Better not; it's a long walk back to Tiffin."

Raymond Sr. had been trying to cut wood with one hand in the side yard. He had dashed away from the approaching car as it made its way down the driveway. Having witnessed its entrance technique to the driveway, he ran toward the house quickly enough to poke his head inside the door to announce the visitors. He tried to return to the woodpile before he would have to do more than tip his hat to the visitors.

Emma Lou saw Raymond Sr. trying to ignore them, but she yelled a "Hally hoo" to get his attention. "Hello, Mr. Huhn." Raymond Sr. tipped his hat to each lady, which required him stowing the ax under his bad arm in order to manage the maneuver.

In as cordial a voice as he could muster, he greeted them, "Good day, ladies." Raymond returned his attention to the woodpile as he added quickly, "The wife is inside." He so hoped that his wife was the object of their visit. Raymond Sr. was humbled by the appearance of these two well-known ambassadors of the church's charity. They usually made visits to the neediest families in the "flock." Yet as he and Georgette had discussed late into the night last night, his family would not help them, so the stubborn pride of the adults should not prevent the children from eating. Hard as it was for him to acknowledge these guests and what they signified, neither he nor his dear wife could come up with any other plan. Their food was running out and it wasn't even winter yet. They had butchered their last pig yesterday. Maybe this was another test that God thought he needed, so he prayed that God would know best and gave his worries up to his Maker.

Ida and Emma mounted the porch steps and knocked on the kitchen door. They noticed everything—the muddy line of mismatched boots at the back door, the sparkling white torn lace curtain at the kitchen window, and the peeled paint and loose hinge on the screen door. They noticed that the door was still a screen door even though summer had left weeks ago. The recent temperatures dictated a storm door would be more practical.

Georgette, Bible in hand, answered the door and greeted them as they crossed the threshold.

Chapter 6

Do-Gooders Arrive

Dear Star,

The barn dance was great. We used old clothes to make a costume for Justin (all the kids dressed as little scarecrows) and all the neighbors got together for a bonfire and corn roast. We drank cider and ate homemade doughnuts and someone brought marshmallows. We toasted this new treat on sticks over the fire—Mom liked hers soft in the middle and then set it on fire before she considered hers done.

Of course I spent most of the party roasting more of these treats for Justin's sweet tooth. It was fun to see the adults dancing. I haven't seen Mom or Dad laugh like that since the accident.

Maybe we will be OK after all.

Elizabeth

Georgette already had a kettle on the stove warming. There was very little coffee and no tea in the house but she had some mint growing in a windowsill pot next to a prized African violet. A bit of mint tea flavored with a sprinkling of brown sugar always tasted good. In spite of the baring cupboards she could muster up some hospitality. "God gave us water for free," she thought as she looked to find something to serve with the tea.

God, her provider, had sent plenty this year. The crops had been good. Yet the harvest timing was off due to the accident. The corn was brought in too late, too wet, and thus brought half the expected value at the elevator by the time the volunteer team of neighbors completed harvesting their own fields and returned to help "the poor Huhn family."

Half price had meant that there was just enough cash to pay the grain storage and seed bills at the elevator and the rent on the land.

So, they had a roof over their heads. There was just very little set aside for food. The usual canning sessions were cut short when the early summer bounty filled all the available canning jars with no cash to buy more jars; they could can with jars only as they became empty. Georgette and the older boys tried to manage Raymond Sr.'s chores. Georgette tried to keep the kids together, pants and shirts mended and cleaned whenever she could catch them not being worn. Then there was the housework. Luckily today it was still relatively clean. Georgette noticed the car and straightened her hair as Emma and Ida made their way onto the back porch.

"The boys must be in the barn," was Emma's first thought after their exchange with Raymond Sr. "Too quiet," she said aloud.

"What was that, sister?" Ida wondered as they walked up the couple of steps to the porch and back door. Reaching for the wood of the door with her gloved knuckles ready for a polite rap, Emma realized that there was no time to answer her sister's inquiry before the door would be answered by Georgette, so she ignored the entreaty and knocked twice on the whitewashed surface.

Georgette swung the door open with a mild smile and greeted her guests. "Come in. Please make yourselves at home."

Emma and Ida obliged and quickly entered the warmth of the kitchen.

"The kitchen is the warmest, or we can go into the living room?" Georgette offered. Elizabeth took that as her cue to add a log to the potbellied stove in the parlor and Justin followed Elizabeth. Justin picked out a log as Elizabeth used her skirt to protect her fingers from the heat of the stove door latch. Once the door was open, Justin handed the log to Elizabeth, who tossed it onto the bright red coals bedded in the bottom of the stove. A few sparks flew out of the open door and landed on the braided rug. In a flash, Justin was stomping on the errant embers in a jig-like fashion as Elizabeth stood back and clapped an accompanying rhythm. The two did this with such a fluid motion that it was well understood to be a daily occurrence. Elizabeth pointed to a spark behind Justin that had missed his attention. He quickly turned and did a two-footed stomp that squashed the spark's oxygen supply forever. Justin bowed as a conclusion to his performance and the two looked up to notice that the adults were in the doorway watching their antics with great appreciation. Embarrassed, the youngsters hung their heads and sat down on the floor with their hands in their laps in front of the stove. They had grabbed what the children considered the best seats in the house, and waited for the adults to settle into the sofa and chair. There were never enough chairs for the kids in this family of six. Early on in their existence the children had learned that their rightful place was on the floor. The adults alone were entitled to elevated seating.

Emma gave a knowing glance to Ida as Georgette entered the living room with Ida. Emma pointed back to the kitchen over her shoulder and Ida nodded her understanding. Ida followed Georgette to the doorway between the living room and the kitchen. As the children settled on the rug, Emma returned to the kitchen and Ida used her bulk to block the view of the kitchen from Georgette. Emma was doing a quick inventory of the kitchen. Emma looked quickly in the pantry—the flour bin was almost empty, there was one day's worth of oatmeal left and a whole bag of brown sugar. The family had a cow, so milk and butter would be OK. There were also a few canned items—mostly tomatoes, a couple of jars of jam—and a whole pig cured and hung on hooks on the beams was the visible protein source.

Emma swiftly moved from kitchen cupboard to cupboard taking notice of the contents and then moving on. A loaf of bread, pickled beets, half a chocolate bar, a jar of honey—and a glance out the window convinced her that the garden was picked clean. Never before had Emma seen a kitchen this stocked for folks in such reportedly poor condition. Maybe Raymond Sr.'s father and stepmother were bringing food in daily. She could relax a little. The Huhn family was going to be OK. The ham and sausages in the pantry would last a few weeks. With Thanksgiving only a month away, she was sure that there would be no want in this household before their seasonal gift baskets were delivered.

Meanwhile the conversation went on in the parlor.

"So Georgette, just how many children do you have?" Ida distracted Georgette's attention from the disappearance of Emma.

"Six. We would have had eight but we lost two boys at birth."

"God works in mysterious ways. Poor Elizabeth, the only girl with five brothers that would have been seven brothers." For someone who had never been a mother once, Georgette was sure that Ida meant well; but the death of any child, even an infant, was a painfully felt loss of what might have been. There is a bonding and great excitement of expectation with every pregnancy. To have lost them at birth meant that a mother would mourn that child emotionally as a loss her whole life. The termination of life with a miscarriage or stillbirth is a painful memory. None of this was evident in the matter-of-fact way that Ida touched the topic. But then she could not be faulted. Life had not blessed Ida with the circumstances that would have led to her understanding of such grief.

Georgette continued as politely as she could, "Yes, Elizabeth has adapted well to her five brothers. She is practically a second mother to the younger ones. Especially Justin."

"Such a good girl." Ida gave a nervous glance over her shoulder to see what was taking Emma so long and was relieved to see that Emma had finally hit the cupboards. "I'm sure you are proud of her."

Emma gently pushed Ida from behind and they both entered the living room together as if Emma had been directly behind Ida during the whole conversation. Emma joined Ida in the parlor satisfied to know that coming empty-handed for today's visit had not been a mistake. They could help this family best by extending the Huhn family food supplies for the holidays as planned. No one was starving here. Emma supposed that someone in the family was helping out. Maybe the townsfolk were too harsh on ol' Burkhardt the German fury and the redheaded angel that were Raymond Sr.'s father and stepmother, respectively.

Emma and Ida talked to Georgette over the refreshing mint tea. After an hour of pleasant chatter, Georgette closed their visit with a scripture reading. The two sisters drove away believing that all was well with the Huhn family. Well, at least until Thanksgiving. Unfortunately for the six Huhn children, the Ladies' Auxiliary visit had come just after the last pig had been slaughtered. Neither Emma nor Ida had noticed that not one chicken pecked playfully in the barnyard. And this was significant; without chickens, there were no eggs, and on a farm these were usually the last to be sacrificed. But one of the children had asked for chicken and dumplings for a birthday supper last Sunday. Georgette and Raymond Sr., in an attempt to keep everything feeling as close to normal for the children as possible, had agreed to cook up the last layer.

Thus Emma's snooping had uncovered a pantry that was deceptively better stocked than it would be by the end of just one week. Neither Emma nor Ida had any idea the quantities of food that six growing children demand. And there were almost four more weeks left until Thanksgiving.

Elizabeth and Justin bounced down the driveway waving "good-byes" to the visitors as the lamb bounded playfully between and around the two children. The three gave the '39 Ford a chase until it turned onto the road. Elizabeth kept Justin and the lamb from entering the roadway, dutifully turned them around, and headed them both back toward the farmhouse once the car was out of sight.

Emma commented to Ida as they drove righteously toward their home, "...and they could have lamb stew next week. I so like a good leg of lamb myself. Lots of garlic and dill."

Ida gasped, shocked to hear her sister say such a thing. "Shame on you. That's a pet. You wouldn't eat your cat if you were hungry, would you?"

"That's different. Cats don't taste good!"

"And how do you know? Why, I was reading about the Orient just the other day and do you know that the Chinese..." Just then the Ford hit a huge rut and the car jostled so violently that it shook the words right out of Ida's head.

Emma sighed deeply. It was stressful enough to ride with Ida, much less to have to also listen to her regurgitate all her reading material at the same time. Emma relied on these deep sighs as her way of releasing that stress onto the world.

Elizabeth and Georgette stood side by side at the kitchen sink and peeled potatoes. They diced the potatoes and tossed the diced pieces into the boiling pot on the stove. Some chopped parsley and butter and cream helped to make a hearty potato soup. The smell of corn bread warmed the whole house. The boys were anxious to be fed and roughhoused in the bedroom upstairs, biding time until they were told that supper was ready. An occasional thump and cry would erupt from the ceiling above the cooks' work area, which never once disrupted their concentration on their assignment with the sharp paring knives. While peeling the potatoes, Georgette's gaze stayed fixed on the frolicking lamb in the yard. Elizabeth followed her mother's gaze. Georgette realized that her daughter was staring at her, and she redirected her attention into a deep returned stare into Elizabeth's eyes. With furrowed brow Elizabeth gently shook her head "no." The message was complete.

The boys were called and Raymond Sr. silently appeared at his place at the end of the table. The soup was served and the corn bread and butter eagerly passed around the table for eight. The meal filled them up and nourished their bodies while the convivial delights of childish chatter and laughter made the meal a celebration of family and a triumph over need. Briefly even Georgette forgot that the pantry was now one meal closer to empty.

Georgette awoke the next morning earlier than usual. She pulled her day dress on over her slip and unbraided her fine long hair, brushed it smooth, and then re-braided it. A morning ritual that ended with the braids looped onto each side of her head, a skill that she had learned to master at the age of seven. She had learned to do this herself for two reasons: one, she told herself, was that this would make her less of a burden to her stepmother, one less duty that the woman would need to perform during her busy day. The more accurate reason was that Georgette's stepmom usually tugged harder than was probably required to get every strand in place. Just one more form of abuse that Georgette could find a way to avoid by becoming independent of this woman's touch.

Georgette slipped out of the master bedroom ready for the day once her face was washed in the basin. She tried to be very careful not to waken Raymond Sr. Healing would be faster with good nourishment and sleep. The sleep was free, but the nourishment worried her.

Once downstairs she stood with her hands on her hips in the pantry doorway surveying her stock. One jar of jam—rhubarb and strawberry—and one of grape jelly graced the pantry shelves. The concord grapevine grew up the side of the porch on a trellis, which was much abused as a climbing rig by her boys. But the vine didn't seem to mind. It blessed her every year with a bounty of black dusty orbs.

These dark treats that somehow were sour and sweet all at once made an excellent grape jam, and only one jar of it was left. The vine blessed them each and every year so far, no matter how cruel the summer treatment by her children had been. This year from a lack of sufficient sugar during the canning time, much of them had become a sour half jelly that the children didn't prefer. Georgette tried mixing it with honey and encouraged them to dip their toast into it. Some would dutifully oblige, taste it, make a face, and then decline it again. The pantry stared back at her, announcing its contents as her gaze ran over the shelves. In her mind she calculated how many meat meals she really had. The ham was worth about ten if she really stretched it. The sausages would do three or four more. The flour would make twenty loaves and it took two or three a day plus one meat meal to satisfy the brood. The only eggs since they had eaten the layer were from an occasional misguided neighbor's goose that would wander over and make a deposit in one of their empty coop's nests and then wander back home. An angel's gift was that goose for sure. The goose had never demonstrated such generosity prior to their coop's emptiness. Usually a good neighbor would return such a stray egg to the owning farmer, but lately Georgette had let the boys bring them to her for a nice change in the menu.

Their breakfasts would be biscuits, toast, or oatmeal, alternated to keep them from becoming bored if possible. They would wash the morning's offering down with milk from the cow. Lunches would be butter or jam sandwiches as long as the flour and jam lasted. Some days she might make a thin ham sandwich just for a surprise. Depending on the wanderings of the goose, maybe even fried egg sandwiches some days. Well, she could keep praying for miracles like the goose eggs and just maybe they would survive. Or if the children could find a hibernating turtle, there might be turtle soup. This late in the year, though, she doubted her luck at this and bowed her head to entreat God's continued kindness. A less devout woman would have been stricter on the rationing. But to do that would, in her eyes, show a lack of faith.

Somehow Georgette made that ham last for nearly two weeks. But that last week before Thanksgiving saw the food run out. The ham sandwiches that she had treated the children with in last Wednesday's lunch boxes might have been an extravagant waste of one supper for this week. Little did she know that those ham sandwiches had been traded for bologna sandwiches from the town kids' lunch boxes.

This morning Georgette was dividing the last loaf of bread into six butter sandwiches, sprinkling each with a dash of salt to add some flavor. The six lunch boxes were packed with one sandwich each and sealed with a prayer, "Dear Lord, please let this fill them until supper. We thank you for the bounty that you have shown us." These prayers were not new. Thanking God for what was contained in her children's lunch boxes was part of Georgette's daily litany of thanks, but the tears were new. As she finished praying over each boxed lunch, she noticed the tears. She quickly wiped them away with shame.

The rude sounds of four waking brothers could be heard coming through the ceiling from the boys' bedroom. Georgette added some more milk to the already thin-looking last pot of oatmeal simmering on the stove. "Well, it will have to do," she said to herself as she put in a bit more brown sugar. She thumped a spoonful of oatmeal into the six bowls on the kitchen table in odd synchronicity with the sound of the children's footfalls on the stairs as the hungry troops descended.

The family members complained or quietly scooped up the oatmeal in keeping with each individual's usual pattern. Justin wanted more sugar on his oatmeal, please, and Doug held his nose as he put each spoonful in his mouth and didn't let go of his nose until he had swallowed. Doug kept this up as an entertainment, one that was being enjoyed by all but Elizabeth and Georgette, until Raymond Sr. came down the stairs, saw the foolishness, and coughed once. He stood there on that last step and silently stared at his brood until even Doug realized whom everyone was watching. Raymond Sr. did not descend that final stair into the room until Doug stopped holding his nose. The children now all silently ate the last few spoonfuls of their breakfast. Some of the children left most of it behind, preferring to be hungry rather than eat oatmeal. Raymond Jr. was in that category. But Georgette assumed that he was man enough at fourteen to decide to be hungry if he so wished.

Within seconds all six children were a flurry of shirts being tucked in, belts being buckled, boots and shoes being grappled over as the boys went for what footwear might fit best as it waited near the kitchen door. Justin had the best selection since the youngest always had the most hand-me-downs from which to choose. Elizabeth chose bare feet rather than wear a pair of her dad's old boots, which were now the only shoes that fit. Once shoed, the children grabbed at old coats, sweaters, scarves, and a flock of mismatched mittens that were in a box by the stove.

Next they lined up for a kiss and a lunch pail from Georgette. She blessed and kissed the top of each head as she handed them their "lunch." The older boys dodged the kiss but artfully grabbed the pail as they whipped out the door. As Elizabeth waited in line behind Justin she glanced into the open pantry and noticed the empty flour sack and the empty pegs where the ham and sausages had once hung. Elizabeth whispered to her mother as her head was kissed, "Mom, what are we having for supper?"

Georgette leaned down and took her daughter's face in her hands and reassured her, "Don't you worry, I have a surprise for you for supper tonight."

With that Elizabeth's brow furrowed even deeper with worry. She looked to her brothers scrapping in the yard with the lamb bouncing around and between them, "But what about tomorrow?" Georgette frowned just enough for Elizabeth to realize further questioning would not be appreciated. "No need to worry about tomorrow either, young lady. God will provide."

Georgette walked out onto the porch clutching at her ragged sweater and pulling it closer around her to close out the bitter late November wind that threatened snow. "No, please not snow," she entreated the heavens. "Elizabeth has gone to school with no shoes—please." Her thoughts rattled in her head so loud sometimes she was afraid others could hear them. She waved at the six who had rounded the corner at the end of the driveway and were headed toward town and school. Now her day would be a battle to find food for the night meal. Raymond Sr. had come into the kitchen and finished the oatmeal rejected by his offspring. Georgette cleaned the dishes as her husband headed out to the barn.

"He hasn't got a clue," she said to her own reflection in the window above the sink as she watched his back heading into his solitude. Only once the children were off to school she sometimes reverted to Deutsch and the sounds she really spoke were, "Er kienst nicht! (He doesn't know.)" These words were said with sadness and a touch of resentment that all the worry was now solely hers. But all was tempered with sympathy for a man, a farmer who lost the function of his hand. There was so much that needed to be relearned, and Raymond Sr. was a man of little patience, especially with himself.

The dishes done, Georgette focused on the provisioning of a meal. She milked the cow and grabbed the shovel. With the implement in hand she headed for what she knew to be a potato patch emptied weeks ago of any more apples of the earth. She personally had made sure that every last potato was resurrected before the ground froze. Now her desperation made her hope that she had missed one or two. Of course the ground threw the shovel back at her with every thrust. Exhausted and defeated, she fell to the ground bent over and rocking with her face buried in her hands.

"Dear Lord, please let there be some food tonight. Please don't punish my children."

Her sobs lessened and Georgette lifted her hands from her face in hopes of finding a miracle. There in front of her was the lamb. "No, Lord, that can't be your answer. Not Elizabeth's lamb." With that plea the lamb gamboled over to the goose that was nesting on a clump of grass nearby yet unnoticed by Georgette until the lamb started the chase. The lamb so disturbed the goose that the goose left its nesting spot and trotted for home, which revealed two large goose eggs in the grass where the goose had been resting. Georgette walked over to the depression in the yard and, still not believing what she was seeing, she looked to the sky. "Thank you, Lord." She picked up the treasures and admitted out loud, "That certainly is a start."

As Georgette gathered the eggs in her arms, she saw an unfamiliar delivery truck coming up the road toward their driveway. As it arrived at the end of the Huhn farm driveway, the driver hit the largest pothole hard. Georgette watched as a huge pumpkin literally leaped from the back of the truck and rolled into their driveway. Georgette secured the eggs quickly on the back porch, almost expecting that the driver of the truck would turn around to retrieve his cargo before she could get to the end of the driveway to claim the gift. But the truck driver was long gone toward the horizon when Georgette reached the pumpkin and carried it back to the house. Head lifted to the sky she all but sang her praise and thanks to her Provider, "Thank you, Lord, oh thank you."

That night Georgette wouldn't answer any questions about what was for supper. Elizabeth was just glad to see her lamb was still standing in the yard when she came home from school. The family was all seated at the table wearing hungry faces tempted by the sweet smells coming from the oven. With a flourish, Georgette took a huge platter of roasted pumpkin pieces out of the oven. She settled the offering on the table next to a pitcher of cream and butter and brown sugar. Every eyebrow around the table was raised at the sheer mound of bounty that was their feast. But Raymond Sr.'s gaze went to his wife with a special attitude of disbelief.

"Georgie, my heavens, where?"

"Exactly," she beamed back as her only reply.

"What?" her husband tried again.

"Let me lead us in prayer tonight." She ignored his second question as rhetorical. As was their usual custom, the family members all grasped hands, forming an unbroken circle as they bowed their heads, and Georgette started.

"Dear Heavenly Father, we thank you for this food which we are about to receive. But most of all tonight we thank you for potholes! Amen."

Raymond Jr. lifted one eyebrow toward his father. A "what's up, Dad, there are no pumpkin patches for miles around here" look, which was exactly what Raymond Sr. was thinking, too. Raymond Sr. just responded to his son's nonverbal question with a shrug and added his ending to his wife's prayer, "Amen, I think."

With that formality out of the way, the hands unclasped and Raymond Sr. stabbed a piece of pumpkin and loaded the creamy wedges onto the eagerly presented plates.

Georgette didn't reveal the origin of their pumpkin supper for years.

That night as Georgette pulled back the quilt to expose her pillow underneath, she was pleasantly surprised to find the festive face of a pansy gazing back at her. Raymond Sr. was already snuggled in the bed. He turned to see his wife's eyes brimming eyes. He patted the bed near him to encourage her to enter the warmth.

"How?" was all Georgette could get out. Then after a few more moments she managed to say, "Where?"

"I am so pleased that you are surprised." He reached out for her and spooned her in next to him.

"How? Where?" were her repeated questions.

"Oh," he wryly smiled his reply, "I have all kinds of little endeavors going on out in that barn."

"I bet you do," Georgette managed a laugh. "Have any extra pigs or chickens stowed away out there, too?"

"I sure wish I did. Maybe eventually we'll need to ask Burkhardt and Patiens for help."

"I sure hope not," Georgette replied. "He scares me to pieces."

"Me, too! And he's my dad. We need not go down that road yet, dear," Raymond agreed. Then, finally, the best friend in times of great troubles came to visit. A deep sleep lay upon them and they rested.

Chapter 7

Empty Larder Days

Dear Star,

I am hungry and worried about food again, mostly because I see the worry in Mom's face again.

I sure hope Mom has something other than lamb on her mind.

God help us.

Elizabeth

The house was quiet, a quiet that only sleeping children can create. The sky was a blue-black backdrop for the icy piercing of the moon's full faced hide-and-seek game that it played with the clouds. The planets and the brightest stars were dancing on the velvet sheeting of night as the blanket clouds tried in vain to keep them tucked in. Georgette could not stay asleep. There was no food left. It was worry, not the moonlit night, that kept her from sleep. She wanted to blame the moon's bright light for keeping her awake rather than worry, for worry showed a lessened faith in the Lord.

She rose from her bed and went down to rock in her chair near the stove. She stoked the remaining coals with a few new logs. The Bible was soon in her hand. Slowly she searched its pages, using the light of the kerosene lamp. She sought solace in the Good Book as the tears rolled down her cheeks and onto the onionskin pages. After reading a few select verses, Georgette closed her eyes and said a silent prayer that she ended with an audible, "Amen."

Hesitantly she placed the Bible back in its spot on the oval-topped piecrust side table next to the lamp and slowly Georgette rose from the rocker, picking up the lamp as she did. Maybe she was already hoping that her prayer had been answered as she went toward the pantry, holding the lamp high to see if perhaps she had missed something. Longingly she looked one last time in each cupboard, ending her search at the last empty cupboard with a sad slight shake of her head. Georgette returned the lamp to the piecrust tabletop, managed her way back up the stairs, and felt her way back to bed. The clock showed eleven as she nestled in next to the snoring Raymond Sr.

When next she opened her eyes the clock showed one. Georgette lay there trying to stare down the moon, which was framed by her bedroom window. The tears streamed onto her pillow, wetting the pillowcase in a damp darkened pool. Even though Raymond Sr.'s snoring was worth crying about, Georgette had become used to it. No, these were tears of a mother's desperation.

"Oh dear Lord, please don't fail me now."

A look of inspiration quickly dried her tears. She mopped up the remaining tears from her cheeks with a wet palm and rose from the bed, attempting not to disturb Raymond Sr. She checked her pantry and cupboards again in a compulsive ritual that would have frightened the family members if they had known just how often she did this each night. There was still nothing in the house to give the children for breakfast or to pack in their lunches. Once she shipped them off to school she had a whole day to come up with something for supper. But that was her existence in the current state of affairs. The few mouse droppings she spied in a dark corner were dried and old. Even the mice had moved to better supplied quarters. There was simply nothing there.

"Answer me, please, dear Lord. I know the Bible says that I should not worry, but if you have no food for your family...Yes, Lord, we could also have no home, be out in the cold tonight, so relatively speaking..."

Georgette's expression changed to one with a glimmer of hope as she said the word "relatively." Dashing to grab a coat and scarf and hat, she tugged on her husband's boots. It was now three in the morning by the mantel clock. She talked to herself as she pulled on the garments. "I can get there and back before anyone wakes up."

The shadow of a woman gripping her wind-whipped clothes as she stumbled and slipped on the rutted and icy driveway made its way down to the road with a path lit by the night-light of God. The figure turned toward town and into the wind. Her wraps were blown about as she struggled against the skills of the wind to chill her. She clutched her coat collar in a determined effort to stymie the wind's attempts to steal her warmth away.

A huge solitary snow cloud covered the moon to give explanation to the fluttering feeble flakes that had just appeared. The three-mile walk took forty-five minutes with the wind making that trip painfully cold. But Georgette now had arrived at the end of their driveway. A driveway punctuated with a rural mailbox marked "B. Huhn." After a brief hesitation Georgette turned into the drive and puffed out her chest and straightened her back, which had been bent to the wind. Model straight, she walked firmly up that driveway to face whatever was there to be faced.

"Thank you, dear Lord, relatively speaking." She glanced skyward long enough to issue her brief prayer of thanksgiving for the suggestion. A suggestion that countered her husband's current wishes. She rarely took action against her husband's counsel but the suggestion from God could not be ignored. She hoped that Raymond would agree with her choice once it was proven to be correct with food for his children. with Almost a smile, one of confidence for sure, she took the last few steps. And then as if pride before a fall, she slipped on an icy patch. The near fall caused her to watch her step a bit more closely, at least until she reached the door. A door owned by a fury of a man, her father-in-law. Her hand, with balled fist, was ready to strike the knock of a welcome entreaty; it reached for the door and recoiled. Her torso turned as if she were considering a retreat. She remembered the redheaded stepmother-in-law that resided on the other side of the door. Georgette talked to her hand as it gained courage to rise from her side and again ball into a fist; and as her knuckles, numbed from the cold, hit the door, she let one more thought escape her lips, "I'd rather eat live mice than beg food from these people, but God has sent me here so I will follow His lead."

Her hand knocked on the door boldly again. She could see that lights were on in the kitchen; a fire flicked warmly, beckoning her with promises of a few moments to defrost. "I'll just ask for their leftover oatmeal"—she didn't want to appear greedy—"and maybe a loaf or two of bread. That will get us through today and I'll have figured out something."

Georgette was hoping that a small request would be hard to refuse.

She was startled a bit when the door was opened. The strong light poured out from the kitchen, which caused her to squint into the face of her main nemesis in life, her father-in-law. "A worse excuse for a man could not have been concocted." The evil thought flitted ever so briefly through Georgette's mind as she laid eyes on this relative for the first time in months. There he was, all of five feet tall and not more than a hundred pounds, but every ounce of him put fear in Georgette's frame. Then this fury of a man slammed the door in Georgette's face, not before some escaping kitchen heat had refreshed her a bit.

Stunned by the slammed door, Georgette stood there on the doorstep for a brief moment. She turned to go when the door was reopened to reveal her father-in-law. He waved her into the kitchen.

"Georgette, come in." He did not stand and hold the door for her to enter. He frowned and walked into the kitchen, leaving Georgette to fuss with the door latch herself.

"Thank you." Georgette stepped into the welcome tropical paradise of the fire-glow-bathed room. Glad to be out of the cold, she drew in the smells that are the smells of plenty. Coffee was brewing in a kettle on the stove next to a huge pan filled with sausages and bacon. The sausages in the pan were singing a sizzle song that sounded like a better "good morning" to Georgette than she had received from the in-law. The pantry door was ajar and Georgette could see hams and sausages hanging from the ceiling hooks. The dictator had taken his throne at the kitchen table where his three hundred pound wife stuffed pancakes and maple syrup and mush into her mouth in great quantities. A whole platter of already-fried meats was resting on the table.

The redheaded Patiens sat at the table and placed a piece of bacon into her gaping wrinkled mouth. She licked her pudgy fingers as she watched Georgette watch her eat what for Georgette was a nonexistent delicacy. Yet Georgette remembered how good their last ham had tasted, and her mouth watered uncontrollably over the thought of the taste of bacon and how the children would love to have a taste, too. Thus swallowing hard before she tried to speak, Georgette created an uncomfortable pause that Patiens felt obliged to smile her way through. Burkhardt leaned against one wall, staring at Georgette and sipping his coffee.

"Speak up, what are ya here for?" Burkhardt barked.

"Well," Georgette struggled for the correct words but didn't know how to speak anything except bluntly so she got to the point. Most of her communications were with children and thus clarity was a valuable ingredient in the orders she would give them. Thus Georgette jumped right into the reason for her visit, with no small talk or well wishing at all. "Since Raymond's accident, it has been hard for him to get work. We are out of food, with six children and all…"

The father-in-law rubbed in the salt as his response interrupted Georgette, "Poor people are stupid to have six children. Should have spent more evenings reading the Bible together."

Georgette's lower lip dropped in disbelief that this man would speak to her in such an indelicate way. Again she tried to gain her self-control. "Think about the children and that long walk home if it is empty-handed," were the thoughts that raced through her mind. Her voice was shaking as she tried to agree with this despicable person, "I know how you must feel…"

Yet she was again interrupted by her father-in-law, "Then why did you come here?"

Her eyes brimmed with tears as Georgette watched the bacon-eater swallow more of the delicious treat and wash it down with a triple stack bite of pancakes and syrup. Burkhardt poured himself another cup of coffee without seemingly a hospitable thought in his body. Never once did he offer her even a cup of coffee and she was too proud to ask for mere common courtesies from these two. Burkhardt watched the two women from his place against the wall with his foot perpendicular to the wall as if a spectator. These were his grandchildren, yet he just stared into his coffee cup to avoid Georgette's gaze of disbelief.

"For your grandchildren's sake," Georgette directed her next pleas directly to Patiens, trying to draw her into the decision, and ignored Burkhardt. "For the children, can I please have some food? Just the leftovers from your breakfast?"

"There won't be any leftovers," Burkhardt offered as Patiens pulled the last strip of bacon from her open mouth and laid it back on the platter.

"Then just some oatmeal or a bag of flour perhaps?" Georgette did not comprehend the totality of their denial. But when her father-in-law walked over to the table and pounded his fist onto the surface of the table with a furious blow to emphasize each word of his next rejection, which would be uttered in German showing his increased level of frustration, Georgette seemed to understand her mistake.

"Aussteigen sie nun (Get out now)!"

Georgette understood that she would get nothing from these people. She would make that cold walk home empty-handed.

Patiens came over to Georgette and gently took Georgette's elbow in her hand as she escorted Georgette to the kitchen door. Burkhardt, whose face now matched his wife's hair color, continued to bang on the table and shout his orders again, "Aussteigen sie nun! Schnell, schnell (Get out now! Quickly, quickly)!"

Georgette turned her back on Burkhardt who had become a screaming banshee; the bacon strip left alone on the platter leaped into the air above the platter with each successive blow. Burkhardt moved toward the now open door and Georgette quickly made her exit into the cold again.

Stunned, Georgette's feet moved without her knowledge as terrible wishes rumbled from the depths of her soul. Hateful wishes. She had made it to the end of the driveway and managed the turn onto the road before she realized that tears were running down her cheeks. Always looking for some silver lining, she reminded herself, "At least the wind will be at my back all the way home." No sooner was the positive thought made than she stepped on an ice patch and landed hard on the frozen ruts in the road. She was now totally defeated. She did not even try to get up. She curled into a ball and sobbed from the physical and emotional pain that the trip had borne her. A glance skyward searched the stars for a glimmer of her God but her tears drowned her view. A few more moments of pondering the frozen heavens and her anger waned some. Praying out loud, she implored her Savior's intercession again, but this time with the help of the brightest star in the sky, which was surely a Christmas star, "Dear Lord, please help me help my children."

A milk truck's headlights materialized on the road be-hind her. The headlights appeared simultaneously with a harsh clap of snow thunder. Under the roar of the thunder, Georgette heard what she thought was the sound of cold tires struggling against what was left of the road. A road that was just ruts and potholes, that was what Seneca County called a road. With the sound of oncoming tires Georgette picked herself up from the frozen surface of the road to avoid being the one soft spot in the road. The truck driver recognized her and stopped to offer her a ride home.

Georgette climbed into the truck slowly, still smarting from the fall, as the driver started to maneuver the truck down the road to her home. The milk truck slowly bounced down the ruts with the musical clatter of the milk bottles chiming in the back. As the driver pulled up to the end of the Huhn driveway, that same bright star that she had hoped was a Christmas star twinkled even brighter as she struggled to wave a "thanks" to the driver—some proper good-bye, which was made difficult by the bread and cheese and eggs and cookies (yes, cookies, too)! Anything he could find in his truck's wares that her cow didn't di-rectly supply was overflowing from her arms. She grinned like she hadn't in days as she snapped open the kitchen door just in time to pack six lunch pails before the first child popped a foot from under his feather comforter and onto the floor.

There was enough food in her arms to carry them two very lean days but somehow Georgette knew that that would be just enough before God blessed them again.

And as she passed out lunch pails filled with cheese sandwiches and cookies, the boys took it as just good fortune. It was Elizabeth who stopped and questioned the probability of it all. Georgette answered her daughter's query with, "God works in mysterious ways."

Elizabeth accepted this explanation without another word. With a good-bye kiss to her mother, Elizabeth was out the door and joined her brothers on the journey to school. It was too cold to go barefoot any more, so Elizabeth limped all the way to school in her too-tight shoes. Halfway down the driveway, Elizabeth's gaze went to the heavens in search of the now fading star.

Georgette watched her daughter's tortured limping progress down the driveway and looked heavenward, hoping for just one more wish to be granted.

"That would be asking for just too much in one day, wouldn't it, Lord?" Georgette realized, and Elizabeth limped on.

Chapter 8

Delivery Day

Dear Star,

It's been awhile since we've seen a full set of three meals all in one day. I keep finding Mom looking in the pantry and cupboards like she is expecting them to miraculously fill up again. We have butter sandwiches in our lunch boxes now. Thank heavens we still have some flour (not sure where that came from) and a milk cow. The lines in Mom's forehead almost never go away.

The meat is gone from the pantry and I am so afraid for my pet lamb, Napoleon. I don't like the way Mom looks at him. I pray that Mom and Dad figure out something soon. There just isn't a lot in the house to eat.

Thanksgiving is coming soon. It won't be the same without a turkey. Maybe Dad can show Raymond Jr. how to shoot down one of those Canada geese. I wonder how that would taste. Heck, in Dickens's era they ate goose all the time.

I better stop writing. I'm making myself hungry. Maybe Mom will come up with another surprise pumpkin supper. That sure was good.

Wishing and praying hard,

Elizabeth

As good fortune would have it, by unanimous vote, the Ladies' Auxiliary had decided that the Thanksgiving baskets should arrive on Tuesday late afternoon in order to give the families time to pluck and clean the turkeys, and slaughter them, too, as the auxiliary had decided to deliver live turkeys. Fresh is always best, and the fresher the better. They had all agreed and live were deemed the freshest.

The auxiliary had prepared twelve "baskets." The baskets were really an attempt not to feed a family for one meal but until the Christmas baskets would be delivered one month later. There were canned hams and sausages as well as whole country hams, smoked chops, and bologna rings. There was a twenty-five-pound bag of flour, ten-pound bags each of oats, barley, and corn meal. Two more laying chickens in a coop for any family without chickens. There were also homemade candies and cookies from the ladies' own kitchens. There were jellies and jams and cake flour, raisins and a ten-pound jar of peanut butter. Each family's basket was proportional to the size of the family, so instead of a peck of potatoes and apples, the Huhn family received a bushel of each. A few loose acorn squashes and three huge pumpkins were tossed in for good measure. Of course, there were sugars and salt and a few basic spices offered also. As one of the auxiliary ladies had said, "In this time of bountiful harvest celebration, there should be no one in our flock who feels that this Thanksgiving is not a time for celebration." Her declaration had been to counter one lady's opinion that they were being too generous. She was worried that they might be spoiling people so that they looked forward to handouts instead of working hard to get ahead. It was the same old argument, with the same weary logic. Perhaps it was time to just agree to disagree. But they had all pounced on this concept, as an excuse to turn away from want; for who of them, in reality, would want to be on the receiving end of these baskets? Placing human pride above the fuel for existence is deadly. Especially when children are involved. Did the children in the Huhn family deserve the fate of their father? In fact, what did Raymond Sr. ever do to anyone to warrant his present fate? The discussions deliberated on the circumstance of each family in their time of need. The final decision embraced by most of the group was that none of these families were lazy or slack. These were good people hit with hard times. And it was up to the churches in the area to help out their own as best they could. Thanks should be given that the Tiffin community had a large heart. There were other communities that instead of helping took the blind eye approach, and good, proud people suffered for it.

Word had gotten around to the auxiliary as discreetly as the milkman could, that help was needed imminently where the Huhn family was involved. Based on this one story, the auxiliary opened their hearts and the rest of the basket recipients were more generously treated, also. But then the need was more deeply felt this year, as hopes that the Depression would lessen wore on weary souls. The world had endured much to make it to 1939 and worse was yet on their horizon. But in the case of the Huhn family, some folks had special resentments based on the apparent refusal of some Huhn family members to help their own.

Ida tried to quote scripture one day during a work session when one of these debates wore on about the milkman's tale of finding Georgette half frozen with despair at the refusal of a grandparent to feed their own grandchildren. "If a family won't help its own, then the church must help. It says so in Luke; yes, that's where that is."

"I think that was Acts, sister," Emma, always the one to believe that she was the biblical scholar, corrected. "What about 'God helps him who helps himself'?" called out the one member who still held out that handouts were a hindrance to long-term survival of the needy—was a better doctrine.

That was when the usually quiet pastor's wife—whom everyone called Miss Lily, not just "Lily," out of sheer respect—piped in to set the record straight, "I don't believe that you will find that one, though often quoted, actually in the Good Book, ladies."

No one would dare rebuke Miss Lily. Why, she had read the Bible cover-to-cover nonstop since she was six, a chapter a day. Miss Lily was one of the most devout readers of the Word to be found in Ohio. The congregation through the pastor's sermons knew this, for Miss Lily would not brag about her devotional rituals. Yet if anyone wanted to misquote the book, she felt compelled to end her normal silence and step in.

"Let's continue this debate with correct biblical references in our Sunday school class next Sunday," Emma suggested. "Right now let's decide how much help to give and be generous about it. That was our decision by an overwhelming majority when we last met, so can we get on with implementing that decision, ladies, please?" She was firm but polite, and work renewed with vigor until all twelve baskets were indeed ready to go.

Some of the members had gone home that night and raided their own family's pantries one last time. They robbed foodstuffs to add to these baskets, making sure that a bountiful and generous message was sent. They were so appalled at Burkhardt and Patiens's denial to Georgette's plea that when the group came back together to finish the process and deliver the baskets, there was twice again the generosity to divide.

Emma eyed the additional offerings. "Rice and macaroni weren't even on the list. You all are so generous."

"It's the least we can do. We have so much sitting on our shelves that we won't miss it," one member claimed.

Meanwhile in her own home, one lady's husband was looking for a new jar of jam when he stumbled upon his own now empty larder, empty except for the note on the middle shelf, "I'll go shopping today—explain later. Love, Mutsee."

Once all the food had been divided up again with the Huhn family receiving the lion's share of this newly found supply, there sat one lonely jar of green imported olives yet to have a family basket. Green olives would be such a rare find in a holiday basket for the needy. The ladies wondered if the Huhn children had ever even had a green olive. "Well, that settles it, then. This jar of Mediterranean delights must go to the Huhn children that they might expand their knowledge beyond the bounds of the family farm." With a flourish the auxiliary lady placed the jar of olives in one of the boxes marked "Huhn."

"All that from a jar of olives?" one lady whispered sarcastically to the closest friend.

The delivery was simple; each lady that had a car had her husband come lift the boxes into their vehicle. Two ladies would go together to make the delivery. The recipients hopefully could assist with the unloading so just the ladies actually made the deliveries. But until the farmer came with the live turkeys, they would all just chat and be patient.

Ida and Emma had the largest car so they would deliver the Huhn basket. Every inch of their car was stuffed with something boxed or busheled or wrapped as a gift or placed in a cellophane-wrapped basket. The addition of the live turkey was going to mean very close quarters. The farmer finally showed up with the live turkeys and all the waiting delivery cars were blessed with one more fine-feathered gift.

Ida's fully packed car drove out of town with Ida at the wheel as usual. True to course, Ida's steering managed to hit every pothole on the road. Emma gritted her teeth, readjusted her askewed hat and glared at Ida with every concussion. The turkey was not too fond of these jolts, either, and pecked at Emma's hat with each new disturbance. Emma yelled each time the turkey nipped her, which started a new round of retaliation from the bird. Emma was pecked again in the process and she reached back to smack the thing with her properly gloved hand, which also received a sharp peck.

Ida could hardly keep the car on the road for all the commotion in the car. "You can't hit an animal like that."

"Why not? They're gonna chop its bloody head off tonight or tomorrow and my only regret is I won't be there to see it."

Emma's hair was a wreck and her hat was atilt as she reached back again, only this time with her purse, and gave the fowl a deserved smack upside the head. This stunned the bird momentarily, then it seemed to recharge its vigor and struck a big peck right on the top of Ida's head.

"Ouch!" Ida was wounded for sure but still was able to keep both hands on the wheel now encouraged Emma as the aggressor and stopped defending the animal. Feathers flew as Emma fought back and Ida cheered for the home team.

"Go get 'im, slugger," Ida shouted out and swerved violently to make sure that she hit that one huge pothole on the other side of the road.

Emma turned around in her seat to face the mean old bird head on and punched the bird right in the gullet. "That's the final straw," she said as she reared back for a forceful punch. "Take that, you stupid bird!" Emma landed the blow, and then another. "You deserve to be plucked alive and cooked, you evil bird."

"And this from the mouth of a Christian lady?"

"Wait 'til he pecks you again, you turncoat."

Now the turkey had more targets than just Emma's hat had provided. Eyeing her as she walloped her purse at him, the turkey took his next shot at her nose. The ensuing yelp and curses that came from Emma settled any doubt that the bird's beak had hit Emma's beak full on. This behavior coming from her righteous sister required comment from Ida. "If Momma was still here, she'd wash your mouth out."

Emma's retort was perfectly timed with another bone-rattling pothole jolt as Emma turned around in her seat to try to regain composure before they arrived. "And if Poppa was still here, he might have a chance to teach you to drive."

Ida almost missed her turn into the Huhn drive as Emma yelled a final threat to the peck at her head from behind, "I'm coming back here to help the Huhn's kill you!"

Noticing the Huhn driveway was approaching quickly, too quickly, Ida slammed on the brakes, sending the car into a sideways spin and slide that stopped with them facing right into the Huhn drive as if by plan. The bird had been badly thrown around and gobbled in disgust. Ida pulled the car into the driveway all slowly and dignified, but the boys had seen her approach on the front road and ran for their lives to avoid collision with the oncoming '39 Ford.

Ida stopped the car with a shudder and a jerk. The turkey went berserk, making the car interior resemble a ripped pillow in a windstorm. As Emma and Ida threw open the car doors and tumbled out of the vehicle to escape any more pecking and flapping, the rain of feathers continued. Ida sputtered a feather from her mouth, and Emma had a few very red marks on her face and one mark on her nose had actually bled a bit, but she didn't know just how badly she looked. She was totally disheveled by this one huge bird. Her hat was mangled and twisted nearly backward on her head.

Georgette, Elizabeth, and Justin stood on the kitchen porch watching with great restrained glee as the two old church ladies tried to regroup clothing, hats, hair, and composure from their indignant auto exit. The two children allowed a giggle or two to escape, and Georgette stopped smiling and whispered a "shh" at them; they toned down their reaction, though with difficulty, to a huge smile.

The turkey was in the back seat gobbling and lunging at the front seat, refusing to admit that the battle was over yet. The sisters continued making attempts at repairs of their appearance that were comically inadequate. But without mirrors they didn't realize that the wisp of hair they thought they were tucking behind their ear was a feather. Elizabeth and Justin chortled again and again; Georgette tried to control her children and herself from offending the ladies. A quick stern eye from Georgette kept these two at least in check. The other four boys had stopped running away from the car now that it appeared to be parked, and approached the car in time to witness the escape of the now-deranged bird from the back door of the car. The turkey ran haphazardly on wobbly legs onto the lawn.

Emma heard the boys shout something about the turkey and she turned to see the stunned animal as it looked for an escape path to freedom. "Get that vile bird! He has been sentenced to death and don't make it a quick one." Emma started to help the boys chase the escapee. Then she quickly realized that the boys were much more nimble than she at changing directions as quickly as the bird did. Emma soon left the turkey trotting to the Huhn boys.

Georgette admitted to herself, "That will keep those boys busy for awhile."

Emma and Ida approached the porch greeting committee, still attempting to correct their clothing disarrays. The boys chased the turkey directly toward Emma and Ida, who ran with terror from it as it pecked furiously at the buttons on the front of Emma's dress. Emma rapped the top of the turkey's head with her purse hard enough to get it to decide that it would rather peck at her necklace instead. Doug finally grabbed the bird by its neck and dragged it away, allowing the ladies to get to the steps. The turkey wiggled its way loose again and Raymond Jr. brought a piece of clothesline into the mix, using it like a lasso. The lamb joined the now rodeo appearance of the capture attempts. Once the bird was lassoed, they paraded it toward the barn, with the leading boy receiving pecks at his heels. Whenever the willful bird attempted to tug against the clothesline to run in some other direction, a following group of brothers would whack it with switches from the willow tree to keep it going in the desired direction.

The first leader received one peck on the heel that was painful enough to get him to drop the line and the bird was free again. The witless bird made a dash for the open barn door. The boys slammed the door shut on him. Full success eventually belonged to the boys. They entered the barn and penned the would-be-dinner in an empty horse stall where it awaited its execution.

Meanwhile, Georgette and the ladies entered the kitchen. "Hello, Emma Lou," Georgette greeted them and held the kitchen door open as they entered. "Ida, good day."

Emma struggled for composure but was still steamed at the turkey. "Nasty bird, I hope he tastes real good."

Ida, also a mess, declared, "I hope all that exercise hasn't toughened him up any."

Georgette tried not to smile at their appearance. "Oh no, we are so thankful that you went to all that trouble. We will enjoy that bird, I assure you." Yet Georgette was really thinking that the meal would have to be pretty good to beat the entertainment value of the animal.

Ida motioned toward the car. "Oh, there is much more than just the turkey; the car is filled." Then turning to

Elizabeth and Justin, Ida added, "Why don't you two start to unload the back seat while your mom and Emma and I talk?"

Elizabeth and Justin scrambled out the kitchen door and yelled directions to the other four. Too late, Georgette howled after them, "Coats! Hats!" Georgette caught a disapproving eye from Emma, which forced Georgette to work to regain her composure, a little embarrassed that she had raised her voice to the children in front of company. She blushed and added, "Oh, it is useless now. I've lost control. Imagine six wild turkeys every day."

Emma gave a noticeable shudder at the thought. "No, thank you, please."

And Ida added, "I can see that you have your hands full."

While the children could be heard loading the kitchen porch with the contents of the back seat of the car, the ladies found some time to talk. The two sisters explained the gift's intent in terms of Christian brotherhood and compassion for a family that just had some unfortunate events occur. These gifts were explained as temporary assistance to get them through the holidays until better times. The ladies and Georgette prayed for healing to come to Raymond Sr. in mind and spirit and body, and for continued faith from the family members. Georgette offered a prayer of thanksgiving for the gifts and the church's generosity.

The noises from the porch sprinkled the ladies' conversation with knowledge of some unsupervised chaos happening near the kitchen door, but they maintained their prayer vigil until the devotion reading was completed. Elizabeth could be heard barking an occasional order, yet the boys were running amok in spite of her efforts to control the mayhem. Now they were playing monkey in the middle with a canned ham, which meant that it was dropped often. They were using it as the football that they longed for but didn't have. Jeffery finally got his hands on it and proved to his doubting brothers that, if thrown properly, you could spiral a canned ham.

When the boys were again serious about unloading the car, Raymond Jr. watched helplessly as Winston, who was carrying a decorated fruit basket, totally destroyed it when Jeffery tackled him at the knees. Raymond Jr. attempted a beautifully executed flying save but was shy of success by three feet. The contents of the basket rolled under the car and the porch and into the ruts of the driveway.

Georgette had gone to the kitchen window to see what was going on and quickly went back to the table in hopes of keeping the ladies from witnessing what was happening to the beautifully prepared basket. "How 'bout we move into the living room for awhile?" The ladies and Georgette moved into the living room as Justin entered the kitchen door munching an apple the size of his head.

"As you anticipated, your generosity is and will be appreciated by everyone in the house."

To which Justin added, through half-chewed apple chunks, "It tastes good, too!"

Emma and Ida both had tears pooling in their eyes and, like watching the fizz in an overfilled glass, one could only wonder: would the tears spill over the edge or retreat back into the container just in time?

"Oh you are welcome, little fella." Emma reached out to toss his hair. Emma reflected on how wonderful it felt to do a good deed. Watching this lad crunch that apple was payment enough for even the time spent with the turkey. But Georgette didn't know that and she felt compelled to add, "You're the answer to a lot of prayers."

There are more important moments in lives, such as births, deaths, and weddings. But right now for the Huhn family, the joy of a full pantry had not been theirs for too long. A full pantry was the most important event a Huhn family member could wish for their family. Georgette had done all she could by herself and one day she gave it all to God in the middle of a frozen road. As a child immigrant she remembered stories of some of the other children who had moved from their European homes because there was little food. But she never imagined such a fate for herself or her children in this new country, nor was she certain that the God she loved was being fair to test her through her children. Georgette had read Job. She knew that all loss was possible when the Almighty turned on his refining fire. The full pantry was rebuilding her faith in God's listening powers rather than his punishing and testing powers.

The next morning, the kitchen at Burkhardt's farm was warm with all the smells of another bountiful American breakfast. The phone rang and Patiens rose with a stuffed mouth to answer it. Before she could rise from her chair, Burkhardt appeared as if a specter and answered the phone. He now stood with phone to his ear, and then he held the receiver out to Patiens who had just happily been spared what she thought was one of life's great labors, talking on the phone. Yet she was not relieved of that chore this time; the call was hers and she would have to stand there to talk on the telephone when it hurt her weight-burdened knees so much to do so.

"If folks had any brains at all, they'd figure out a way to get that thing to let go of the wall!" she complained as she chewed and talked and wobbled her way to the phone. "This better be good." Burkhardt handed her the phone and left the kitchen. Patiens was always happier when Burkhardt left her alone. If he weren't in the room she wouldn't become his next target of abuse. She put the phone to her ear as she picked some bacon from between her teeth with her fingernail. She inquired into the mouthpiece, "What do you want?" There was a pause as the caller answered but was probably interrupted with Patiens's next statement, "What do you want to know for?" The caller was again given a small window of opportunity for explanation before Patiens spoke again, "Well yes, she did come here begging."

In another kitchen, about a hundred miles south in Kettering, Ohio, was the caller. A slight woman in her early thirties was speaking with great patience no matter what Patiens said or how she said it; "Howard and I were concerned that they were getting enough help. So what happened?"

The other end of the conversation confessed, "Burkhardt sent her home. He was outraged at her audacity to make her six kids our problem."

Back in the Kettering kitchen, Emily covered the mouthpiece of the phone and shook her head in the negative to Howard who sat with a cup of coffee. He lowered his head and released a huge sigh. Emily vigorously waved Howard to take the phone. She was so disturbed by Patiens's last comment that she would rather Howard be the one to talk to his mother. She let go of the phone and before it hit the wall or floor, Howard jumped up and caught it. Emily stomped away to do the dishes that waited in the sink.

"They are your parents," she whispered as she walked to the sink half-hoping that Patiens would hear her. "You deal with them. I can't."

"Hello," Howard started. "Yes, Mom. Oh, Emily had to answer the door." Just as Howard had uttered the words, Emily turned on the disposal in total defiance. She watched as Howard tried to cover the mouthpiece quickly enough to protect his lie. She was pleased by the trouble she had caused. Her delight was evidenced by her laughing smile. Howard stepped up to her challenge and though flustered a bit, he let a loving grin appear ever so briefly because his sympathies were clearly with his spirited wife.

"You were saying about Raymond, Mom?" Howard nodded to what must have been said on the other end of the phone but said nothing else. He just listened. The conversation was one way as most of his parent's conversations were. Emily left the room shaking her head as if she were a horse that had flies buzzing its ears. Her dear husband suffered the buzzing silently. Howard was a respectful son whether his parents deserved the respect or not.

Chapter 9

Justin's Wish

Dear Star,

    The boys all went sledding and I am sewing with Mom. Gosh I love to play in the snow but it is so cold out, I would have to wear dad's boots and Ray has those.

    Oh well. Hope they treat Justin OK without me there to protect him.

Bored but warm,

Elizabeth

    All the way to town the six children silently watched as Winter's white toys bounced off invisible hands. A huge wind swept across the road in front of them, washing the air fresh. It was Sunday and the Huhn children were thrilled with the prospect of sledding the afternoon away. Sledding until their bottoms ached and their bellies yelled for lunch. Sunday's lunch would be more than what the past few Sunday lunches had been. With a full pantry, they had pancakes for breakfast with turkey sausages. So lunch was bound to be even more spectacular than that.

Elizabeth didn't plan to join into the sledding plans. No shoes and no boots meant that she would be left behind. She would make some excuse to stay in so that her brothers wouldn't feel guilty that she didn't join them. Justin would feel guilty and would probably volunteer to miss a wonderful time if he knew she didn't come along because she didn't have any adequate shoes. At least Justin would care. They would do whatever they wanted regardless of the feelings of anyone else.

But first things first on a Sunday, and that meant church services. All six of them tramped into Sunday school as if some unheard general had shouted the orders. They bounded their way up the church stairway to the loft where four of the Huhn brothers made spit balls out of "Upper Room" pages and sent them flying at the teacher's back or Sandra McGinnis's curls, whichever their fancy chose.

Elizabeth took Justin by the hand and led him to his Sunday school class. She then left limping for her own class. Emma and Ida gladly took Justin under their collective and ample wings. They exchanged sweet knowing smiles when he entered looking very happy and well fed.

"Breakfast was good today, Justin?"

"Yes," he naively answered. "I had syrup on my pancakes as thick as I wanted."

A knowing smile of self-satisfaction warmed Emma's cheeks and Ida dashed a tear away as she pretended to turn to the desk to shuffle some papers with no real purpose.

Emma had all seven of the four- to five-year-olds seated at tables. She started the instructions for the day's lesson. "We are going to draw Christmas presents today."

Ida passed out the construction paper and added, "Does anybody know what the first Christmas gift was?"

Hands went up all over the room. Ida called on Shirley, a redheaded little spitfire with pipe curls just like her older sister who was upstairs and the object of torment of Justin's older brothers.

"OK, Shirley, what was the first Christmas gift?"

Shirley responded in her most perfect imitation of her idol, her older sister, "Everybody knows that. Sure…frankincense, gold, and myrrh." She nodded a snotty punctuation to Justin as she completed her answer. Justin had planned to play the same role as his brothers with the McGinnis sister, but Justin planned his attack from an intellectual level.

Emma saw Justin's eager face and figured that he did have the better answer. "OK, Justin."

Justin beamed from ear to ear but at the teacher, not at Shirley. Elizabeth had taught one of her brothers manners, Ida thought, as Justin answered so assuredly.

"I was told that the first Christmas gift was the Baby Jesus. 'God gave his only begotten son to the world that whosoever believeth in him should not perish, but have everlasting life. John 3:16.'"

Emma and Ida looked amazed and shook their heads in delighted agreement. Ida answered with a huge smile of pride. Proud she was to be this child's Sunday school teacher.

"Very good, Justin. Yes, that was the very first Christmas present. The Baby Jesus was the gift that God gave the world. The gift of a baby through whom we are all promised life everlasting."

Shirley was giving snotty looks to Justin throughout this acknowledgment from the teachers. But Justin just drew a sketch of his planned Christmas project.

Emma Lou continued the lesson.

"So every year we give gifts to one another as part of the Christmas tradition."

Ida came in as if on cue, "I'm sure some of you have Christmas wishes."

"Let's go around the room and each of you can tell the class what you are wishing for most this Christmas, Let's start with you, Shirley.'"" added Emma.

"I want a dollhouse, a real china tea set, new ice skates, a new muff, a doll carriage..." As Shirley mentioned each item, she held up a sketch for her classmates to see.

Ida interrupted the narcissistic litany of greed, "Oh, that's nice..." And she motioned for Shirley to sit back down. A command Shirley actually took seriously and promptly did just that.

Emma switched to Justin in hopes of a more inspired list and she was not disappointed. Justin held up a picture of a pair of lady's shoes. Some of the children began to giggle before he could explain.

Emma attempted to get clarity. "What do you want most for Christmas, Justin?"

Justin answered still very sincerely, "New shoes for Elizabeth." Another knowing look passed between the two spinster sisters. Then Emma and Ida dueted a response, "Oh, that's very thoughtful, Justin."

Emma leaned in to whisper to Ida, "Make a note of that one."

Ida responded as sweetly as she could, "I did, oh I did."

Emma pointed to the next child as Justin sat down, "And you? What do you want most for Christmas this year?"

Chapter 10

Christmas Plots

Dear Star,

Wishes do come true. The pantry is as full as it's been in weeks. Still no new shoes, but I believe Christmas will change that. It simply must.

Justin has started to talk nonstop Santa Claus this and Santa Claus that. Mom has given me the responsibility of keeping my older brothers from spoiling the Santa part of Christmas for what might be Justin's last "magical" Christmas. With the big mouths on my brothers this will not be easy. Justin has started saving bits of paper and string for us to use to make some ornaments for the tree that he so anticipates. Even the string that Mom used to tie the Thanksgiving turkey's legs together was washed and donated to Justin's cause.

I look forward to having children of my own someday as long as they are like Justin, what treasures they will be.

Elizabeth

The sky on this cold late fall night was as if glitter had been scattered on black velvet. Other worlds that singed the mind with imagined intensity, sat in their own neighborhood so far away and beamed down on this small reflective orb and its inhabitants. The car was as silent as a 1939 Studebaker could be. Emily prayed and wished on every star she thought had twinkled at her. A prayer that someday she'd have a child for whom she would prepare all sorts of Christmas surprises. Teach that child all the ways to celebrate life and the birth of the most blessed Child ever. Unlike the Virgin Mary's miracle birth, the doctors had failed to find a miracle for Emily.

Howard wondered what could have his dear wife so quiet. She wasn't an unusually gabby lady, but this level of silence had him concerned. He knew how hard the holidays were on her, or at least imagined that for a woman, his own longing for offspring must be magnified. The feminine clock and its hormonal tickings were not a pressure on him except through his wife's desperation. He reached out for one of those folded lilies that lay gloved in her lap. Smiling with a fearful look of intruding, Howard quizzed his wife, "Penny for your thoughts."

Emily startled a bit at the sound of his voice. Then she smiled feebly and replied, "You know we have to do something."

And like a good husband he searched his knowledge of this fine lady and worked his mind methodically through every subject that could have taken her mind from thoughts of her longings. With the slightest of hesitations he joined her topic.

"Why didn't they ask us to help?"

"Pride?" came her one-word reply.

"A brother ought to be able to ask a brother for food to feed his offspring. My own niece and nephews...I would not have declined."

"Maybe they are a little gun-shy after the 'warm' reception your parents gave them."

Howard could sometimes be a little defensive of his rough-edged parents. Emily described them as selfish to the core and this from a woman who was generous to a fault. That and many other lovely qualities were exactly why he chose her. So on this one topic he usually allowed her excess and he didn't defend them tonight. For even the respectful, dutiful son had found this latest episode hard to understand. How could a grandparent refuse to feed his grandchildren? Granted, these children were not his mother's grandchildren, but still they were his father's grandchildren.

"So what do we do now?" Howard was ready for suggestions. He wanted to help but he didn't want to hurt his half brother even more by hurting his pride, too. The question was too weighty to expect an immediate response. The silent drive continued as he and his wife looked for a solution. The rumbling of the suspension interrupted the peacefulness of the night as it complained about the pitted farm road.

One star winked suggestively at Emily and it held her attention. Emily wished on stars and prayed to them daily for a daughter or a son, but a daughter to shop with and spend time with would be so wonderful. Maybe they could find one in an orphanage for a couple of weeks for the holidays—she had heard of people doing that. Yet that seemed so insincere and unfair to the child as much as it would be heart-rending for her. Then, startling a bit, her face exploded with the excitement of an excellent idea. Howard noticed the change.

"Well?" He hoped to entreat her to share her thoughts.

"I know what we can do."

"Please, share, dear. The suspense is killing me." Howard laughed at her enthusiasm. His voice smiled back warmth as he watched the animation in that face next to him. In fact, he was witnessing a level of animation that he hadn't seen from her since they were young lovers.

"First we send a letter to Georgette," Emily clasped her hands together in delight. "We find out what they want and need and we can make a Christmas for Raymond's children."

Howard nodded in agreement and opened his mouth to acknowledge the idea when more came pouring from his spouse. Every time he tried to interject one of his thoughts, her face would light up anew and out would come more elaborations on how she thought this whole Christmas project should unfold.

"We make Christmas for them. We can have the fun this Christmas that people who have children get to have."

"Maybe some year…" Howard tried to make it a conversation. But Emily did not wish to have his sentence finished. She held her hand up to force a finish to that thought before it could tarnish her present happy mood. She did not want to shift back to her own gloomy plight. Instead she wished to remain focused on the vision of the Christmas Present that she had painted in her head.

"This year we will be happy with the Christmas we give."

Elizabeth had no idea the ripplings that her mother's begging trip would bring. An event twice blessed. Like a prayer twice heard. That cry Georgette had shouted in her cold desperation in the frozen ruts of that Seneca County road had bounced off some heavenly body and into Howard's car. Emily heard the prayer that God had already chosen to hear and Emily answered it as bountifully as He had upon His first hearing.

Chapter 11

A Christmas Letter

Dear Star,

I wonder how poor we really are. The only food I've seen come in the house has come from the church ladies. We've had no visits from the landlord and Mom lately ends every prayer with, "Thank God for the roof over our heads." So we must have paid the rent on the farm. Mom and Dad say nothing so I just hope all is gonna be OK for a good Christmas for Justin and the boys.

Worried,

Elizabeth

The after-supper hours, when the dishes lay again peace-fully clean in their cupboard, the glasses all stood sparkling and at attention and glittered through the glass panes of the china cabinet, and the cutlery was tucked safely out of harm's way, these were the moments that belonged to Georgette. Her brood was scattered around the farm sup-posedly doing chores or more likely just playing in the barn away from the bitter winter winds. These were the hours that she was allowed to be alone. It was a peace that lay on her day like lace on a mantel. Ever so beautiful, yet the weight of it gave no evidence to the impact that it had on her soul—purely a miracle.

Georgette picked up her worn Bible and began to read. Then she remembered the letter. She rose from the rocker to retrieve the letter, which she had laid down in the kitchen, setting it aside for this time of the day. The post had come just before supper and the house had been a zoo. Now she could enjoy its contents, for she had taken just enough time to notice the return address and knew that this would be a gift of some sort. That's just how those dear souls were.

On returning from the kitchen, letter in hand, she glanced at the stove and wondered if another piece of wood would be wiser than to let the room become chilled. Deci-sion made, she placed the letter on the piecrust-topped table and selected a few small logs and gave them a toss into the belly of the stove. She opened the door and closed it by bunching her skirt into her hand as a makeshift potholder just as Elizabeth had done. Assured of warmth now, she settled back into the rocker, raised her reading glasses to her nose, and opened the letter.

Carefully she pried the contents from the lovely boxed-stationery envelope. As she opened the envelope and unfolded the pages, she ran her hand across the embossed pastel bouquet lovingly, appreciating the finer details of life that currently were beyond her means. The letter popped out with something that fell into her lap. It was a self-addressed stamped envelope back to the senders—her brother-in-law and sister-in-law, Howard and Emily. Georgette smiled sweetly at just the memory of each of them and eagerly unfolded the letter.

That night while cuddled into Raymond's loving arms, Georgette shared the contents of the letter with him. While initially he was trapped in his own selfish pride, Georgette eventually showed him that it was also a decision to be made for everyone else involved. She mentioned the joy of their children who otherwise would have no gifts. Georgette's assumption pried from Raymond Sr. one of his barn secrets.

"Georgette," he said in earnest disbelief, "our children would have had a Christmas without Howard and Emily's generosity. The hours spent in the barn—what do you think I'm doing out there?" he ended teasingly.

"Honestly?"

"Yes, dear."

"I've been worried that you were brooding over your loss."

"Well, silly girl, first it is OUR loss. What happens to one of us happens to both of us. Second, brooding is the furthest from my efforts in the barn. Mainly I've spent that time trying to relearn some skills. Each child will receive a small handmade gift from us. Which, compared to the gifts I'm sure that Howard and Emily will bring, will pale in comparison. Probably get lost in the gift wrap. Might be best to save them for some other time."

"No, dear. The exact opposite is needed."

"What, decline Howard and Emily's offer?"

"No, I was referring the homemade gifts. It might be a reassurance to the children to see what you can still do in spite of the injury."

"Yes, I can see that as a worthwhile effort, but back to the other part of this. You know how much I hate charity."

"Raymond, you will be giving as much as they are. You will be donating your family to them; allowing them to be Santas will be the biggest gift you and I could ever give to them. They know how proud we both are. They will appreciate us letting them do this as much as we will appreciate their giving spirit."

"Right as always, dear." He gave a deep sigh. "I give in."

"Oh, thank you, dear. I have finally convinced you, then?"

"Mostly dear, I figure it's the only way I'll get any sleep at all tonight."

They both giggled a bit at Raymond's silliness, then cuddled back into one another's arms.

That night Georgette lay ever so still until she heard the soft rolling of distant thunder sounds that signified a sleeping husband. She gently removed herself from his arms and bed and headed for the piecrust table to write her acceptance reply.

Chapter 12

The Reply

Dear Star,

I showed Justin Orion last night and he again pointed out his favorite twinkly star. I can't write too much. I've been working on sewing a stuffed animal lamb for Justin's Christmas present and I only get to work on it on clear nights after he has fallen asleep. And tonight is a perfect night.

Santa,
Elizabeth

The stars in the night sky were dancing for Justin again. He liked to call it dancing even though Elizabeth insisted that it was twinkling, not dancing. There didn't seem to be that much difference to Justin, so around Elizabeth he tried to remember to say "twinkling." Justin lay on his back watching the morning stars, his favorite part of the winter mornings. He would stay all tucked in so that the tiny pocket of warm air that his small frame could generate would not be lost while he watched and sometimes talked to the stars. This was Justin's precious time of the day. This morning he was making Christmas wishes to the stars and with every wish that Justin sent up to the star today, it danced back at him. He was sure that this was notification of receipt. The dancing was the star's way of saying, "Wish received and acknowledged. Delivery can be expected."

As Justin watched the dawn brighten the sky, a honking mass of geese wiped across the bedroom window. The memories of southern breezes must have fueled their vaga-bond desires. It was the largest group of geese that Justin had ever seen or heard. There were maybe twenty or thirty Vs, a battalion of birds all getting an early start on the day's journey together. The geese now gone and the dawn light growing, Justin turned back to the business of making Christmas wishes on the stars before they faded into the brightness of day.

His child's mind still believed that all wishes would be fulfilled if that receipt acknowledgment were given. His smile broadened as he closed his eyes and mouthed an al-most breathless wish. He opened his eyes quickly and watched for the star's response. The star did dance. Testing the limits of his luck now, he wished one last wish with all his might, and then quickly opened his eyes to see if that wish "got through." Yes, the star was dancing as vigorously as ever. Justin was grinning like his face would break. He was laid out like a happy drunk, eyes closed with his head on his pillow, when Elizabeth walked in.

"Hey you!" she said, made curious by the deep grin on her littlest brother's face. Justin startled and opened his eyes but he was still grinning like the Cheshire Cat. Curiosity caused her to quiz him closely but with a teasing smiling countenance. "What's on your mind?" She was now starting to get serious, because he had just ignored her after the original startle, closing his eyes again and lying there grinning even more. "Justin, are you OK?" Now her tone was of a worried nature and she watched as his face grew sober and she felt badly if she had caused his obviously joyful state to end. Then softening her tone again, she sat on the bed next to him.

"Hey buddy, what's on your mind this morning?"

Hearing from her tone that she wasn't mad at him, his smile instantly returned as he rolled over still under his covers; facing her and now smiling sheepishly, he gave his reply, "Just making Christmas wishes."

"Now that you brought it up, what are they?"

"I can't tell you that. It would break the spell."

"OK …keep your secrets to yourself, but we do have to go to school today. At least a few more days and it is Christmas break. So get up!" Elizabeth flapped his covers around him, letting gusts of colder room air chase away the warmth of his cover cave and taking away all reason to tarry any longer. Squeals of shock peeled out of Justin who finally jumped out of bed and scampered to the basin to wash his face.

"I've laid your clothes out on the bed for you already. Now hurry or you won't get any pancakes."

"That's OK. I just eat them to drink the syrup, anyway."

"Not in this house, you won't!" Georgette poked her head into their room, trying to make the morning schedule work, and overheard enough about Justin's plans to drink the syrup that her mother switch was thrown. While Justin buried his head in his sweater, Georgette handed a letter to Elizabeth.

"You wouldn't mind mailing this for me on your way to school, would you, please?"

Elizabeth took the letter and glanced at the address and became quickly animated. "Aunt Emily? Are they going to visit?"

Georgette smiled a broad smile that faded quickly to her usual furrowed brow. She shrugged and bit her lower lip to keep from saying any more.

Elizabeth fingered the beautiful embossing on the stationery envelope, touching each flower gently as well as the names on the address. Her fingers touched the embossing with great respect and affection, as if to caress their names would be to caress the very people for which the names stood.

"Oh, I hope to see them again. I do hope that they will visit."

Some of the worry washed from Georgette's face to hear her daughter say those words. Georgette reached out to pat Elizabeth on the back and kiss the top of her head. The surprised look on Elizabeth's face attested to the rarity of this gesture, usually done only once a day on their way out the door to school. Elizabeth figured it was just a touch of the Christmas spirit that had her mother so sentimental.

All six children bustled at the back door, fighting over the best mittens and hats and grabbing for footwear that would suit the snow depth as best they could. The six lunch pails were all provisioned well enough—in fact, better than would be expected for a family in the shape that they were in. Thanks were given daily to the Ladies' Auxiliary. The four older boys departed the kitchen with the usual wrestling and punching. Yet Justin waited for Elizabeth to hold out her hand for him. The kitchen door slammed shut, which was the way the house said its good-bye to the older boys. Collars were quickly turned up against the cold for those who weren't fortunate enough to win the scarf tussle. One gloved or mittened hand held a lunch pail and that same hand also held their collars shut against the wind. The other hand, usually bare, was stuck deep in a pocket.

"Don't forget to mail the letter," Georgette called out from the kitchen door held wide open.

"I won't, Mom, you can trust me," Elizabeth answered without turning her face into the wind.

Georgette remained at the door, waving to their departing backs. Justin turned around and waved his lunch pail wildly back at her, banging the pail against his arm as if it were a free gate in the wind, smacking the fence.

Winston was wishing he were a girl so he could have a matching pair of mittens. He was not happy about the arbitrary favors that the only daughter seemed to always get. Doug was wishing he were younger so that he would get two mittens or two gloves also. Getting older was not a great experience. Double digits for him this year and he would give one digit back for a second mitten right now.

Elizabeth offered her second mitten to Justin when she realized that he had lost out with the older brothers and again was given only one mitten even though the family rules were that he would get two. She inspected her brothers ahead to figure out who had done Justin wrong. She quickly figured it out when a nicely packed snowball smacked her hard on her left cheek and nearly took her hat off from the backlash. Only a two-mittened brother would be making snowballs that tight.

"Ouch! Jeffery, don't pack them that tight—that hurts," she yelled after the mitten thief. Yet she knew that any instruction given to this one was a waste of breath. She'd watched both her mom and dad give up on words and just send him behind the barn with his dad for a few lashes with the belt. It was the only thing Jeffery seemed to respect.

Elizabeth held the mitten coaxingly in front of Justin's face as she wondered why girls were demanded to be so tough yet also they were supposed to be soft and feminine at the same time. A mitten offering to a younger child while the offerer's hand was numb with cold seemed maternalistic—a tough role, she had decided. Justin finally took the mitten and with that hand grabbed hers and stuffed both of their hands into her pocket to get them out of the wind in hopes of lessening the pain for his sister. Someday she would meet someone who would take her to her feminine side and she'd never need to be tough again.

Chapter 13

The Best is Yet to Come

Dear Star,

I can hardly believe the behavior of Mom lately. She's been acting excited about Christmas. She and I even helped Justin make some decorations for the tree last night. Hints were dropped that the tree might go up earlier than usual this year. That would be the bee's knees.

Hopeful,

Elizabeth

The sound snippets of an ax hitting its mark came through the curtain of snow that bounced like a host of white moths cavorting at a lamp on a summer eve. Yet the two inches of snow already on the ground spoke not of summer but of an early, pre-Christmas winter. The steps of the chopper were fresh made in the snow and the lamb bounded along behind them looking for some company, which was quickly found. The ax work done, Georgette dragged a tiny-looking spindly evergreen behind her. She smiled back at the lamb's friendly gaze.

"Hello. Have you come to see what all the fuss is about?" Georgette lugged the ax and the tree diligently like any pioneer mom would have. She concentrated hard on the task of managing the tree up the back porch steps as she talked to the lamb. "This, my little fluffy friend, is a Christmas tree. Your ancestors were there at that very first Christmas, weren't they? And I just bet that somewhere in that little lamb pea brain you know that." The lamb tilted its head as if remembering some long implanted history that was rooted in his very genetic material.

Georgette was focused on maneuvering the tree up onto the porch steps and the lamb came up the steps, pausing as Georgette, having mounted the steps, opened the kitchen door. The lamb stopped at the opened door, afraid to over-step the taboo of the kitchen door threshold but longing with every look to follow that tree inside. Georgette couldn't resist that plea-full look any longer and for the first time ever she let the lamb come into the kitchen. It shivered at the instant warmth and cautiously watched Georgette take the tree into the living room where there was even more warm air. Too much warm air, thought the wool-encrusted lamb, at least too much for a lamb that could not take off its coat and put it back on like the humans did.

With its nose pointed toward the living room, the lamb stood with its body still in the unusually cooler kitchen. Georgette had let the kitchen fire die down a bit. She had built up the parlor fire instead, in an effort to warm up the area of the house where she would be working on the tree. The lamb stood there for a while, watching the shadows and shapes as they played on the parlor walls. He eventually curled up on the kitchen floor as the unusual warmth of the house lulled him to sleep.

Raymond Sr. had fashioned a crosspiece of two fir strips nailed together as a stand, which Georgette nailed to the bottom of the tree. Miraculously, the tree stood tall and straight on the first attempt to raise it. Raymond Sr. sat in the chair next to Georgette's rocker and watched her progress with the tree and never offered to assist when three hands would have been better than two. He seemed to think if he couldn't offer to make the total four, then why offer. But his comments he did offer, thinking perhaps that he could reduce the work she was doing by encouraging her to lower her standards rather than offer assistance. "Isn't it a bit early for a tree?"

Georgette started her thought all right but choked back the tears halfway through it, "This may be the biggest part of the Christmas celebration these children get this year. Let's let them enjoy it."

Hours later the feisty five boys rushed in from school with their shepherdess losing any battles at the rules of behavior. Especially when they saw the tree. The heady smell

of pine in the house and the thrill of the season and anticipation of decorating the tree required restraint and these
boys had none. Coats and gloves were dropped where the
boys stood. Boots and shoes were not allowed go to more
than three feet beyond the kitchen door, much less enter the
living room, were flung off as each boy rushed to be the
first one to plop down in front of the tree and just stare at it.
Naked as it was of decoration, it didn't matter. The tree was
in the house. The holy shrine of Christmas hopes had been
erected in the parlor. And the children would worship in its
shadow until the rituals of Christmas bore the fruits of the
season—Christmas gifts.

The snow kept right on falling as the children's excitement mounted. The thrill of the season, which had now
been officially confirmed with the appearance of the Yule
arbor, was bursting at the children's very seams. The flurry
of activity brought the lamb from a dark corner and Elizabeth ran to hug her new indoor pet. Burying her face in its
fleece, Elizabeth noticed that her mother was soaking it all
in.

"Can he stay inside just one night? Maybe Christmas
night?" Elizabeth was astounded by her own brilliance and
bounced to her mother for an answer. "Please Christmas
night?" Georgette had to turn her back to hide the tear as it
slid down her face.

"Why not tonight?"
"Really?" Elizabeth couldn't believe her ears.
"Well, we do have tons of stuff to tell him about Christ-
mas. This Christmas is his first."

Georgette finished popping some popcorn and took it into the living room for the boys. The boys attacked the bowl and one another with their needles and thread, and they munched and strung the kernels while Elizabeth and Georgette tried to scrape enough ingredients together to make a batch of cookies. The remnants of the treasures that were brought by the Ladies' Auxiliary for Thanksgiving were running low. There was still a week until Christmas and the arrival of the promised second basket of the season would be delivered before that day, but when exactly wasn't known.

"Will we make it?" slipped audibly through Georgette's lips and into Elizabeth's anxious ears. They both stood in the nearly empty pantry. Elizabeth cuddled the lamb that rarely left her side. Hearing her mother's renewed concern over food, Elizabeth drew the lamb closer to her side in a protective maternalistic way, a gesture not wasted on her mom.

Georgette made a pledge she knew she might be forced to break. "Don't worry, dear. He's a pet, not a meal."

But it was a long time until Christmas Eve, the traditional day that the Christmas baskets were delivered. Georgette had stretched that pantry before and she was bound to make it last again. "Even if we have scrambled eggs and eat one of those layers, we will make it without cooking that lamb." Her thoughts were interrupted by the noise of a brotherly ruckus coming from the other room. Georgette went into the parlor sensing that something was going terribly wrong with the tree-decorating efforts. Elizabeth and the lamb were left alone in the pantry as Georgette left the kitchen to referee in the tree room. Elizabeth buried her arms around the lamb's neck and they snuggled into one another's hair—Elizabeth with her nose against the lamb's wool and the lamb nuzzled his nose into her hair. And there they sat. Contentment and peace reigned well in the Huhn house that night; well, at least in the pantry it did.

Chapter 14

Premature Delivery

Dear Star,

How I wish for a pair of warm mittens for each of us at Christmas. Warm boots. I should have made Justin mittens, not a stuffed lamb. Shame on me for not being more practical.

I worked with Justin on his Christmas play part and he was all secretive about his Christmas gift. He's working on something but he won't tell me about it. Wonder what it will be.

Aunt Emily and Uncle Howard will visit. I love those two so much. Always candy for Justin and a toy for the boys, a bracelet or barrette for me—always something for everybody. Mom says it's because they don't have children of their own. I mailed a letter to them from Mom a few days ago. The stationery was so beautiful—the flowers weren't just printed on the paper, they were raised up off the paper somehow. Mom called it embossing. Someday I'd love to have a beautiful box of stationery like that.

We have empty shelves again. For supper last night we had one handful of popcorn for each of us. A week until Christmas and we have almost nothing to eat again. So to keep from thinking about being hungry, Mom and Dad let us put up the tree earlier than usual. We put up the tree, one we cut from the meadow, and decorated it with popcorn and Justin's homemade "ornaments." His ornaments were made with the foil from chewing gum wrappers, sticks tied together to make stars, and food cartons cut and folded into bells. Tin can lids crimped by Dad during one of his barn sessions really made some plausible star things. Justin had also made paper chains with colorful magazine pages and we used them all.

Hungry again,

Elizabeth

It was a week before Christmas and already winter had blessed them with a thin coat of snow and a perfect frosting of ice glazed most roadways. Ida held the wheel of the black Ford sedan in a death grip, peering through the top of the wheel rather than over it. She was bobbing her head like a strutting rooster as she worked to get a decent view of the road ahead. She was doing her best to pilot this craft from a

stature-disadvantaged position. The car had been manufac-
tured with a mature male driver in mind, not a battle-weary
spinster.

Ida did manage to continue her record performance of
being able to find and hit any decently sized pothole in either lane. With each disturbing jostle of the vehicle, Emma
Lou deposited a disapproving acknowledgment in Ida's direction. Emma Lou could bite her tongue no longer and felt
obliged to make some quip in return for the latest teeth-
shattering bump. "Is it against the law to miss just one pothole?"

Ida, indignant at the shot, put up a defense that took her
attention from the road ahead. "For your information, if I
swerve to miss a pothole, then I'd be left of center."

"So?" Emma replied while she watched the road ahead
more than Ida did.

"Well, that would be against the law," Ida replied with
airs of supreme knowledge about the topic of driving. Ida
was still not watching the road as much as she was watching Emma. The '39 Ford started to drift toward the ditch
that ran parallel to the road. Emma could take Ida's inatten-
tion no more and she grabbed the wheel to save them from
the watery ditch.

"It's only against the law if you are caught. Now watch
the road."

Ida was flabbergasted at such an attitude and huffed a
reply, "That's a hell of a note!"

Emma gasped in disbelief, "That mouth!" She shook her
head in shocked reflection and pointed her index finger di-

rectly at her sister's nose and shook it at her with every syl-lable. "Heaven help you."

Ida got her last shot in before she decided to drop the battle as pure futility. "And you, too!"

There was a brief silence while the two sisters cooled off and tried to regain that mutual respect that had kept them close throughout the years. The Ford sedan continued to crunch its way down the road and Ida turned on the radio to fill the unusual silence. Generally speaking she drove to match the tempo of the music, so this was not a popular move if there were other drivers on the road. She was going much too fast for the road conditions now that the song had changed from "Silent Night" to "Deck the Halls." Another hard jolt of the car set Emma Lou off again.

"That one sure would'a shook up that turkey."

Laughing, Ida added, "Don't remind me of that nasty bird."

"Yep...this time we were smart."

"Yes, we were. A dead bird can't peck." They both smiled and shared a mutual nod toward the back seat. There was a huge basket filled with at least a week's worth of food, including a fully dressed twenty-pound turkey.

Emma still laughed at the memory of the Thanksgiving bird. "Yep, those potholes had that bird so mad he didn't know which way to point his pecker."

Ida gasped in utter and total shock at her sister's mouth again, "Why Emma Lou Snodgrass!"

Emma tried for a what-did-I-say look, and then hesitated as if remembering what she had just said, and when she did remember she quickly slapped a hand over her mouth. "Oh my," she exclaimed, and laughed with Ida, "Oh my." Emma gave Ida a startled look. "Why shame on you, Ida, for thinking of such a thing."

The car continued dashing down the road too fast to safely turn into the Huhn driveway. Ida slammed on the brakes and the black sedan slid sideways until the car rested with its grill pointed straight down the Huhn driveway.

Emma white-knuckled her grip on the overhead handle and just shook her head in utter disbelief. "How do you do that?" Ida just beamed, thinking that she had been given a sincere compliment, and concentrated on moving the car down the driveway with the same reckless disregard for the safety of anyone nearby as she showed anyone on the roads of Seneca County.

Raymond Jr. had been in the yard building a snow fort when he saw Ida get that car to slide right into position like a wheel man in a mob movie. He whistled to his brothers, who were out and about the farm causing trouble instead of doing errands. "That would be a safe bet," Raymond Jr. thought out loud. Raymond Jr. chose a particular whistle that the brothers had concocted as a special emergency signal and the brothers scattered for cover. This signal was dubbed the "Dad's home" call since most of the time when they were in any danger; it was from their father. It was a whistle that might just save their behinds from some duly required discipline for some horrible wrong that that day had brought.

It was a whistle that had them run and hide behind a preselected outbuilding. They usually stayed hidden until Raymond Jr. whistled an all-clear signal. Each brother chose a different outbuilding to hide behind. Dispersion would mean that their dad would be able to catch hopefully only one of them. That unfortunate might be the only one to get a whopping. It worked sometimes.

Not hearing an all-clear whistle, they stayed hidden for a few moments. Once the brothers had nerve enough to look out, they saw that the car was that '39 Ford that almost ran them down at Thanksgiving. They slowly worked up enough nerve to come out of their hiding spots but fully understood why Raymond had chosen the "Dad's home" call. That's the only warning that might have them scatter quickly enough to save them from the seemingly out-of-control car that was shooting down the rutted driveway.

Emma punched home one final shot at her sister's driving skills, or lack thereof, before she had to be all pleasant in front of the children. "Are you sure that's the way you are supposed to turn?"

Instead of answering her sister and risking an escalated argument in front of the children, Ida started singing along with the radio, in a voice that could clear a ball field, "We Wish You a Merry Christmas." Emma eyed her sister closely then added to the musical mayhem and sang along, too.

The sound of the car crashing down the drive alerted Georgette, Justin, and Elizabeth to peer out the closest window by sweeping aside the curtain. Something they knew was rude and unrefined, but it sounded like a son/brother could be in jeopardy, so all manners flew out the window. Georgette chuckled slightly, then cleared her throat to set a better example for the children. She quickly returned to her stern look and frowned at their joviality. Elizabeth and Justin barely regained their composure by the time the boys had scampered away and the car was safely stopped. "Until the keys were out of Ida's hands, there'd be no real safety," Georgette caught her less-than-kind thought, then instantly repented, "Shame on me."

The mother and two indoor children headed to the back door to be ready to greet the guests. Georgette took one look at the lamb and another at the calendar. They were a whole week ahead of Christmas, God bless those Ladies' Auxiliary sisters. How did they always seem to know? Supper the night before had been a handful of popcorn each—"party food," Georgette had called it. Her glance went closed eyed to the floor as she gave thanks to the real One who knew the timing perfectly.

Emma and Ida hopped from their car and shouted hellos to the still-escaping boys. The sisters slid on the slick surface like kids up to the back porch steps. The boys soon gathered and started removing the food from the back seat of the car with great enthusiasm. The huge basket with the turkey passed from hand to hand until the last pair had control, much like a bucket brigade. This continued in a fairly orderly fashion until all the boxes of food and even some wrapped gifts had emerged. More gifts than any of them had thought would be possible this year. The boys relayed the items to the back porch, and then Georgette, Justin, Elizabeth, and the sisters managed to get everything except the canned ham into the kitchen. The canned-ham football game was renewed and all degrees of silliness erupted.

Georgette couldn't stop thanking them the whole time the sisters transferred the food into the warmth of the kitchen. God bless you's and Merry Christmas's were exchanged around the room in a bubbling up of excitement. The boys came in to get warm after just a few moments of "the game" but Georgette knew that it was really to see whose names would be on those gift boxes. The boys rushed into the house, each one bound to be the first with his coat, shoes, and hat stowed before he could get his bottom on the floor next to the tree. Good seating was always important in a large family. As Georgette and the sisters brought the gifts in from the kitchen and placed them under the tree in the parlor, Justin's eyes lit up brighter than a Christmas candle. His eyes followed each delivery of the beribboned packages to their spot under the tree like a puppy watches a treat. Once all the boxes were under the tree, the boys rushed back to the kitchen with some mission in mind and Justin followed with the lamb. Elizabeth stayed behind seated with the ladies, trying desperately to be one, too. Justin eyed the baskets and boxes as if he were looking for something in particular then came back into the living room; having remembered the fun of their last visit, he blurted out his question, "Did ya bring another wild turkey?"

Georgette's face was tortured with the look of motherhood, never knowing what your offspring might say next. Yet the sisters were drawn to his excitement and they stooped to his level to answer him. Emma started, "Yes, Justin, we did bring a turkey…" With that as his whole answer he tramped off as if a popcorn out of its prison, yelping his questions as wildly as that old tom turkey had gobbled. "Where? When can we get him?" He jumped at the window in hopes to see if the bird was still caged in the car.

Ida ran to the huge basket sitting on the kitchen table and pulled back the linen cloth that covered the contents to display an enormous bird, plucked bare and cleaned. Justin turned as they lifted the veil and his head hung in sadness at the lost frivolity and stated the obvious, "It's dead already!"

"Yes," Ida agreed, "this one is dead already."

"We learned our lesson with the Thanksgiving delivery," Emma added. She exchanged glances with Georgette and Ida apologized for the obvious disappointment that their prudence had brought to Justin. Justin headed back for a spot near the tree, no longer as interested in this reappearance of the Ladies' auxiliary.

The other boys started to look a bit glum, too, when Ida remembered that the trunk was still full of items. "Why don't you children go unload the trunk for us? I think that there are more presents and maybe even some candy left out there." The sweet tooth of the family, Justin, was no longer wearing a long face when he heard about the possibility of candy and Ida had known that. She was his Sunday school teacher and Sunday school teachers often learned a lot about their small charges. She pulled the keys from her purse and lifted a questioning brow to Georgette who helped out.

"Raymond, why don't you lead the boys?" Raymond beamed as he reached out to accept the set of car keys. One of the few times he had felt that magic in his hands. The other occupants of the room did not, but Georgette noticed that this was a special moment for her oldest and she watched every move on his face. The younger boys were tussling over coats, hats, boots, and gloves when Raymond caught up with them at the back door and went out without anything added but his boots. Georgette watched from the window and shuddered visibly when she saw that the other boys had gone out without much else on.

The back door slammed, signifying each new load of treats that entered the house. Georgette tried to distract her guests from this bustle. "Tea or coffee?"

"Oh, that is so gracious, Georgette, but we do have another stop to make yet today." The children had regrouped under the tree with faces alight with wonder. All those Christmas presents under their tree, Ida and Emma beamed at their triumph of generosity. Georgette escorted the ladies out the door and watched to make sure that they were safely in their car. She waved good-bye from the kitchen window and shouted a Christmas blessing to them, "God bless you both and a very Merry Christmas."

Georgette pulled her sweater tightly around her against the cold. When the car started to back down the driveway, she surrendered to the cold, waved one last wave of "thank you and good cheer" and went in to the warmth of the kitchen. The door closed behind her and she stood stunned at the silence of her home. She was amazed at the quiet of her expectant children. The silence didn't last too long as the children started to grapple over the gifts. Georgette headed into the parlor to referee. She grabbed a box from Winston who had just grabbed it from Justin. She smacked Winston in the ear with what felt like a sturdy box. Yes, she thought, it was sturdy enough to get a yelp out of Winston as he reached up a protective arm to ward off any further blows. The reaction was what she had hoped for: a settling of the uproar.

"Give that to me," Georgette ordered. "What seems to be the problem here?"

Raymond Jr. acted as spokesman for the boys. "It looked like it could be a football," he said almost apologetically. For a fleeting moment Georgette wondered if these boys might turn out all right after all.

Always hopeful, Justin gave his vote, "It's a fruitcake." Which got "yucks" from everybody else.

"You and your sweet tooth," Doug fumed at Justin.

"Yah, well, it's sure no football," Justin shot back.

Georgette stood in silence, tag in hand, not believing her earlier thought. There appeared to be only one real present. All the other "presents" were bundles of food well beribboned. So these six children were all focused on the one football-sized box.

Georgette ended the debate. "Tag clearly says, 'To Elizabeth—Open anytime before Christmas.'"

"Cripes," shouted Jeffery. "Only one girl in the family and she gets the only present."

"Go! Enough!" Georgette waved her arms and hands over their heads like a duck flapping her wings over her ducklings, "Go! Do your chores. Go help your father in the barn."

The boys dodged her and scrambled to the door.

Georgette tried again, "Coats! Hats!" but with little real effect. Some grabbed a coat, some a hat, only two grabbed both. "That wasn't a choice." Faceless hands reached back in for a hat or coat once the wind hit them. She caught the door to prevent another slam and gently closed it behind her. She watched them dash to the barn. The lamb bounded behind Justin. It was so happy to see Elizabeth outdoors. Georgette leaned her back up against the door again and looked to the ceiling. "Thank you, Lord."

As Georgette unpacked the food boxes, she turned to hide some nuts and oranges in the butter churn. "Not much but that may have to do as stocking stuffers this year."

She finished packing the food gifts in the pantry then settled in her chair to read her Bible. The children's chore time always gave her that needed moment to gather scraps of her soul and knit herself back. Barely in her chair, she spied the gift under the tree. Georgette jumped up, grabbed it, gave it a quick shake, and then ran back to her chair before she could be found out. Ashamed at her childish inquisitiveness, she fussed at herself, "I wonder where the children get it?"

Now all adult-like, she opened the Bible in her lap. She closed her eyes. With the lines of deep prayer creasing her forehead she moved her lips to speak words so softly that only the One to whom they were intended would ever hear them.

Chapter 15

The Shopping Spree

Dear Star,

The pantry is full again. We children are all back to discussions of Christmas wishes again. Funny how food is our focus if there isn't any. Once some shows up, our priorities quickly revert to less practical matters.

Justin's stuffed lamb is done. It is blue eyed and has a ribbon around its neck for a leash. It is so cute if I do say so myself. I made it from scraps of an old white chenille bedspread.

Oh, there is a package under the tree with my name on it. It looks like a shoebox! Mom and I made cookies to hang on the tree for more decorations once the Ladies' auxiliary brought us the Christmas basket of goodies, and my present.

Excited again,

Elizabeth

There would be no spirit of Christmas without music.
God even provided music for that first Christmas, the finest
heaven could provide, the singing of angels. For surely that
demonstrated the proper celebration of His Son's birth.
Aunt Emily caught herself humming along to the songs as
the piped notes slipped through to the sidewalks of Day-
ton's fanciest retail streets. Uncle Howard picked up his
wife's tuneful timekeeping with the current carol. His eyes
twinkled and an approving smile touched the corners of his
mustached mouth as he slipped his hand around hers and
his step almost became jaunty and so did hers to mock or to
just appreciate his enthusiasm. He enjoyed the song and
their perfect rhythm down the street, until, that is, he was
bridled up to the Tidekey's window. The holiday-decorated
window was complete with a Santa's rear emerging from
the fireplace. The window was finished off with a fair-
haired lass asleep on a huge recliner, still dressed in her
Christmas Eve finery.

Howard studied his wife's face to see if he could fathom
the reason for this sudden stop. It appeared that she had focused on the child. As her eyes teared, he lost his smile.
Yes, that was the pain of a childless union. The ever-
present topic was clearly mindful again. Sobered, he waited
for her to move, letting her work through the emotions before they discussed it again. That approach might be the

best, he reasoned. Howard really never knew if his choices of how to handle these moments were wise. He prayed often that he would be led to find the best means of support for his and her grief. A gentle squeeze of her hand on his was a signal that her trance was over.

"What?" he inquired with the gentleness of Freud with a child.

"I have to have that."

"I know," he started to say but stopped himself. Her disposition was so chipper, she couldn't be upset in any way. Best to wait for more input, maybe then he would unravel the mystery of the female mind. She pointed at the child now with a big smile on her face.

"That dress."

"Oh," was all he could exhale along with a sigh of relief. Anything his wallet could fix was an easy fix for Howard.

"I have to have that dress for Elizabeth!" she added. She teared up again with what Howard surmised was the joy of anticipated giving.

"Let's go get a price then," he volunteered as he dragged her willingly with him into the same revolving door compartment. They tumbled into the store giggling like school kids. They ignored the looks of the more serious shoppers who for some reason seemed annoyed at the sound of laughter. Maybe these disgruntled shoppers had figured out how to leave the Child of Christmas alone in his manger, undisturbed by the joys of the season. But the stoic's way of celebrating was far from the spirited wisdom of these new entrants.

Only a few minutes elapsed and these two emerged back on the street. Emily had a long face and Howard tried to be supportive. Their arms contained no more presents than when they had entered the store.

Howard huffed his issue out into the cool air of the sidewalk, "That's highway robbery."

A disappointed Emily agreed, "It is such a pretty dress," her resolve weakening a bit as she planted herself in front of the very same window which housed the little girl in the recliner scene. Emily stood and stared at the scene again. Howard sidled up to her and waited there next to his wife. He also stood staring at the dress with her, waiting patiently for more input. Instead of talking, she tilted her head, first in one direction, and then the other as Howard mimicked her every move. This was strictly a way for a very bored man to be as patient as possible with his lady. She took one last glance at the dress and then she made her request one last time with only her eyes.

"Now wait one minute," Howard gently started. "We agreed not to get too lavish."

Emily turned from his gaze and directed hers back onto the dress. "Yes, we did."

Howard worried again that good sense was being re-placed with emotion and stated his case once more. "They need the money for food more than a fluffy piece of velvet-een."

"You are so right, dear."

But Emily understood the importance of a piece of vel-veteen fluff when you are thirteen and have never had any of the finer things of life.

Howard was very worried now, for how could the logic of a husband ever win over the emotional judgment of maternal instinct? It's simply not supposed to, he guessed. "So?" was his only reply. He decided right then to let go and let the decision be hers. How would he understand what that dress might mean to a poverty-stricken thirteen-year-old girl? Men should probably be overridden in matters of the heart more often than they are, he rationalized. Only a man would choose the belly as more important than a fancy dress.

"So?" He tried again to fetter out what they were doing.

"So, what?" was her inquisitive and calm reply.

"So, why are we still planted here in front of the store window, dear?"

Mildly mocking his semi-annoyed tone, yet with a lovingly huge grin she explained, "So I can memorize every detail and sew her one, dear."

Relieved and chuckling at how she could play him, he mocked back, "Very wise choice, my dear." They clasped free hands together and strolled toward a bell-ringing Santa. The tinkling bell created a Pavlovian reach of Howard's hand into his pocket and he retrieved a few bills, which he gladly dropped into the bucket. Santa's eyes popped. He was familiar with the nickel-and-dime contributions of some folks or those who pretended to be blind and deaf just for his block.

"Merry Christmas, sir." Uncle Howard nodded to the Santa as he dropped the few bills into the open kettle.

"And a Merry Christmas to you, too—oh, a great jolly one to you, sir."

"You ol' softy." Emily grabbed his arm and gave it a big squeeze. She beamed a smile up at him. Still so pleased, after all these years, with the choice she had made as an almost child bride.

"I can afford to be generous. You just saved me ten times that amount."

The two flew down the street as if they were newlyweds, their feet barely touching the pavement. Just when he thought they were finally headed home, she pulled him into a toy store. Emily tugged Georgette's letter from her purse, consulted it, and bought a football, which she instructed the clerk to wrap. Emily and Howard browsed through the toys together, then apart, and then together again like a slow-motion reel that separates and reunites the couples throughout the dance. Finally, Howard stopped by a beautiful black bike and wheeled it over for Emily's approval. She squealed with excitement, causing the shopkeeper to eye these two very carefully. "Too many drunks this time of the year, spending next month's paycheck on toys, when most of 'em can't even afford to eat." But that craziness was what put food in his kids' mouths, so the shopkeeper would take a sale even from a couple that had been "hittin' the bottle."

"That's top o' the line, folks. Very nice choice."

Emily shook her head but left the decision to Howard. This was certainly his territory.

"We'll take it," Howard gave his verdict and then delivery instructions to their home soon followed.

Emily and Howard waltzed out of the store and Emily showed her approval of the bike purchase. "Getting in the spirit, are you?" Howard smiled back brightly, revealing a heart as big as his wallet.

Chapter 16

Some Lofty Ideas

Dear Star,

I forgot to thank the dear Lord above for the Ladies' Auxiliary. Without them, I'm sure Napoleon would have been a meal by now.

The boys shake my present daily, even though it is not for them. Their sheer joy that there is any present under the tree is understandable. For a present under the tree for one of us bodes well for the others. They know how fair Mom and Dad always try to be. Never would one of us get something on Christmas and the others get nothing. So they guess that they must be getting something.

The war in Europe is on the radio news. We heard of some news. Many Jewish people have already come to the United States rather than stay in Nazi-overrun Europe. Our teacher says America will be blessed by these great minds that are joining our country. I hope that she is right.

Elizabeth

No finer playground was ever conceived than that of a barn filled with hay bales, the square ones. These were the best building blocks for forts and tunneling ever made. The tackle and ropes made it easy for little monkeys to swing from one loft to another. But once their energy was measured out in the construction, it was customary to hold adult-free councils to discuss world issues and upcoming events, like Christmas. Even children can solve the world's woes while surrounded by the sweet aroma of hay and straw and tractor engine oil.

Justin and Elizabeth had nested with the lamb in their fort, waiting for the boys to finish theirs, which was usually built with one design feature in mind. That being how well it tumbled when they jumped on it when the inevitable moment of implosion arrived. The lamb bleated every time Elizabeth shifted her weight for fear she was leaving its side for a higher loft. This for the lamb would be an unwanted event; it had happened in the past and it greatly upset the woolly wonder. The only way the lamb could reach the lower lofts was by climbing and hopping on the tractor. To get any higher, he had to rely on Elizabeth to carry him. That had worked when he was very small but now he was just too heavy for her to lift, so he feared getting left behind.

Elizabeth and Justin were unaware that the other loft occupants were making a sneak attack via belly crawl. The
increased silence in the barn should have been warning
enough, since the only good Huhn brother is usually the
one you can see and hear. The quiet meant that either they
were plotting some terrible deed or executing one of those
plots. The final few feet of the attack was made with much
of their favorite play ingredient: noise—wailing, and
whooping.

Jeffery tackled Justin and Winston took Elizabeth.
Jeffery held the lamb at bay. The lamb protested greatly not
for its own discomfort but to protect Elizabeth who was
making more noise about the hay being stuffed under her
clothes than she ever had in the past. The lamb kicked
Winston after learning that a similar move had freed it from
Jeffery's grasp. One good punch with a hind hoof and
Winston had a red hoof print on his temple for days. But he
did let go of Elizabeth. Winston rolled in the hay dazed and
rubbing his head. The lamb gave him a parting shot to the
shinbone, which was marked by a sharp yelp and an ago-
nizing fetal roll as Winston admitted defeat. "Uncle! Get
your blasted lamb off me!"

Just then Jeffery left the Elizabeth fight and jumped on
Justin who Doug was not terrorizing with nearly the proper
amount of gusto. With their release, Elizabeth and the lamb
went to defend Justin. By now he had had more than
enough rough play and was in tears. Elizabeth pulled
Jeffery off and peeled him to one side where the lamb kept
him at bay.

"You bully," she yelled at Jeffery. "Pick on someone your own size." Elizabeth cuddled the straw-stuffed Justin in her arms until he stopped crying.

"He is my size," Jeffery snipped back. By height that was almost true, but Jeffery outweighed Justin by twice the pounds and Jeffery was all muscle. The invaders sulked off to lick their wounds before their implosion event. They required some time to recharge and regroup before they had the energy for any demolition work.

Elizabeth tried to find a more pleasant topic to occupy the mind of the youngest brother as they pulled straw out from under their clothing.

"So what do you want Santa to bring you, Justin?"

Justin surprised her with his comment. "He's not coming."

"What?" Elizabeth's favorite brother was becoming a skeptic, too!

"Jeffery says he's not coming."

Elizabeth turned to frown at Jeffery who couldn't hear their conversation yet knew from his sister's accusatory and furrowed brow that he was being blamed for something by his little rat-fink brother whom he would plot something against someday when Justin was not the baby of the family. His mom could always add a few more babies to the nest, which would make Justin fair game overnight. Jeffery ran to shout from the edge of his loft, "What? I didn't do it."

Elizabeth lodged her complaint. "You told him Santa wasn't coming." She leaped to her feet and faced Jeffery from her loft, nothing between them but a ten-foot drop to the floor and twenty feet of tractor-filled barn.

"Hey, Dad hasn't worked in months—not since the accident," he yelled across the void and then ran back to his fort while screaming his final prophecies at them from his fort's summit, "There are no gifts coming to this house this year."

Justin's eyes were filled with tears again as Elizabeth took her place in the hay next to him. Justin hung onto the seasonal story as best as he could against what his older brother was saying and he repeated his arguments aloud through his tears, "But Santa makes the toys, not Dad."

Jeffery defiantly hit Justin with his inexhaustible verbal cannon, "Grow up, baby!"

Elizabeth guessed the next line that might come out of Jeffery's pie hole and threw out her warning, "Don't you dare, Jeffery!"

Winston exited the older-brother fort to stand next to Jeffery and throw his opinions forth, also. Elizabeth knew that there would be strength in numbers, so she covered Justin's ears and started singing "Deck the Halls" at the top of her lungs as the brothers yelled nearly in unison, "What? Tell him that there's..." The rest of their shout Elizabeth successfully drowned out.

The boys stopped yelling when Elizabeth grabbed the rope and swung over to their loft on the rope and tackle. She chased them down, threw Jeffery in the dungeon of his own fort, and decked Winston with a haymaker that landed him on his backside. Winston folded over and gasped for air, as the sucker punch had been more forceful than she had intended. Doug was surprised that she had defeated two brothers and was now focused on him. Doug tripped and she tackled him as he attempted to escape. As she sat on him and pulled his arm behind his back, she never stopped her inquisition, "SO, Doug, what do you want Santa to bring you?"

Doug started to say something else, "There is no such..." and Elizabeth yanked on his arm even harder. Something her brothers had taught her and now she thought it was high time to return the lesson on them. Doug yelled in pain, which kept Winston and Jeffery fairly quiet since they had never heard or seen Elizabeth this physical before. The tormentors were now showing fearful respect of what she could really do to them if she wanted to. "I'll ask again and again, Doug, and each time I will increase the hardness of my pull. So what do you want Santa to bring you, Doug?"

Doug turned his head and hissed at Justin and Elizabeth, "IF there was a Santa." And Elizabeth almost dislocated his shoulder with the next tug, which created a yelp that sent chills up even Jeffery's spine. Justin started pleading inaudibly for Elizabeth to stop. But she demanded one more time, "What do you want Santa to bring you, Doug?"

Doug could not take one more tug on his arm so he finally gave his older sister what she demanded, and his answer was "a football."

Jeffery finally regained his spine and yelled at his brother from the dungeon floor, "A football? Come on, the sky's the limit here. There IS a Santa. What would you ask for now?"

Quickly Doug and Winston in unison bellowed their heart's desire, "A two-wheeled bicycle. Black. Squawk horn. Handlebar covers to match." Like a mantra they had all memorized, they shouted out their Christmas order. They all knew every detail. They wanted the exact same visual picture. There was probably a fingerprinted page marked in a Sears catalog, under a bed on the second floor, was Elizabeth's guess. She released Doug. She was satisfied that he had said under torture what she needed Justin to hear. Her job was done for this year.

"Yah! That's the way. Think big," she encouraged.

"With mud flaps."

"And a chrome mirror."

"Yah," said Winston. "Good one."

"And a basket for the front handlebars," Justin piped in.

"You put that basket on your tricycle, but keep that kid stuff, girl stuff, off'n our bicycle, ya little maggot." Jeffery's mean-spirited reply had Elizabeth up and moving. She did not approve of the misplaced venom in his voice. She had had enough of the older brothers for one day. She kneed Jeffery from behind, which rolled him into the hay and off the loft, dropping him to the barn floor. Miraculously he missed all of the obstacles that could have seriously wounded him. But instead of more than a peering down to see if he was still alive, Elizabeth ranted on.

"I can't believe you guys; now you are fighting over something you won't ever even have. You disgust me."

The two older boys looked to one another with an inquiring look—that look that just maybe they had pushed someone too far and they knew it. Just might be time to run for cover.

Elizabeth grabbed Justin as she collected the lamb to carry it out of the loft. "Let's go, Justin. Next they'll be arguing over who gets to ride it first." And that did start them up again, just as she had predicted.

"I do, of course," Jeffery shouted to the backs of the three silhouettes that were framed by the opened barn door.

"No, I do," hollered Winston as he tackled Jeffery down into a fresh pile of straw.

The retreating three ignored the shouts and tussles that came from the barn. Justin reached up and grasped Elizabeth's hand as they walked to the house. The lamb was on her other side as she took her credits, "See? I told ya so." Justin just nodded in knowing agreement.

Justin tugged on her hand to stop her, his usual format. For deep thoughts he liked to slow down to a stop and face her so he could read any nonverbal reactions on her face. For as young as he was, he had already learned that in those reactions lay the truths that the words might try to shield from a small child. "Is there a Santa, Elizabeth?"

Elizabeth tried to turn her face away from Justin's inquisitive stare. She was sure that she knew exactly why he had stopped their progress; she reached to pet the lamb as she crafted her reply. She ran her fingers through the thick wool of the lamb, then turned her face to look directly into Justin's eyes as she replied, "I believe in him. Is that good enough proof?"

Justin nodded in the affirmative and gave Elizabeth a huge smile that he saved for very special moments. She squeezed his hand in reply.

Once Justin and Elizabeth were inside, Georgette called for Elizabeth to help in the kitchen while Justin continued into the parlor. Drawn like a magnet into the room that held the tree of wishes, he stopped to revere it. He closed his eyes and imagined the room loaded with many wrapped packages plus a black and chrome two-wheeler sitting in the corner and an obvious wrapped football under the tree inside a chrome basket that was just the right size to be mounted on a tricycle.

Justin continued to stand there, eyes closed, as Santa walked up from behind him and reached over to pat him on the head. Santa mouthed the words, "Good boy." Then reality returned as Justin opened his eyes and the imagined gifts popped from his view as if they were balloons tickled by a pin. The only gift under the tree was the one to Elizabeth from the Ladies' Auxiliary.

He whispered as he knelt to worship the one gift of Christmas in their entire home, "I wonder what it is?"

The one star, Justin's star, twinkled brightly in the night sky just outside the window that framed the tree, as if it was a treetop ornament from the heavens.

Chapter 17

Helping Hands

Dear Star,

    It is Christmas Eve morning. And it's Mom's birthday. I made her a lace-trimmed card from some of Justin's saved ornament scraps. I plan to give it to her at breakfast. If I am burning with excitement how is Justin coping!

Off to bake cookies! More later if I find time.

Merry Christmas,

Elizabeth

The oven was going full bore, making the kitchen even warmer than usual. The oven did a fine job of chasing the drafts back from the chilly cheeks of winter's start. Coming into the kitchen on a winter's morning was like stepping back into life itself. Again the family had survived the night chills of the bedrooms. Bedrooms like these were why feather beds were invented—and down comforters, and woolen pajamas, and bed jackets, bed warmers, hot water bottles, slippers, and so on. Rooms that were so cold in the dead of winter that the washbasin water would have a skin of ice on it in the morning. Mom would still expect you to wash your face and hands in it before you could come out of that South Pole existence back into the tropical zone of the kitchen and living room.

As each child entered the room they wished their mother a happy birthday and gave her a hug and a kiss on the cheek. This was such an unnatural act that Georgette was sure that her daughter must have orchestrated this display of affection. As Elizabeth hugged in turn, she handed the lace-trimmed card to her mom.

"Thank you, Elizabeth. It is lovely. Simply lovely."

The children gladly grouped into the kitchen with Georgette on a normal day, but today, Christmas Eve morning, was so special. The anticipation was palpable as the children watched their mother bustling from stoking the oven to beating ingredients in bowls. Next she would be whipping out orders to one child to go see if those lazy hens had laid another egg yet for the pie that was about to be completed and placed in the oven if ever the current resident pie was baked. All this urgency kept them busy preparing the big feast that was Christmas Eve. Whenever possible, it was a feast at the Huhn family farm, and this year it looked particularly splendid.

Georgette usually only went to this much fuss for guests. The children saw hints that there might be guests for supper tonight. There were three pies, not two. Two pies would mean just the eight of them for the meal. But three pies were the first clue that the children had that there might be more mouths to feed than usual. Isn't it amazing the information a mind can calculate from pie? There was one each—pumpkin, pecan, and mince. The mince was all for the adults, as not one Huhn child would even try it. Justin wondered why there was no cherry pie, which was his favorite.

The pies were laid to cool in the parlor, whose stove fire was just coals early in the day. The living room stove would be stoked later in the day to actually warm the room if company was coming. The cookies would be baked next. They were mixed already and sitting in the icebox to harden before baking. The six children were at the table eating mush, toast and jelly for breakfast. Mush was not a favorite but Georgette had set out brown sugar and maple syrup for the holiday, which made it edible. Besides, there would be plenty of treats later in the day to look forward to, so even Justin gagged down his mush without the usual complaining.

Georgette darted from one chore to another in a greatly organized kitchen ballet. Now that she had the last tray of cookies in the oven, she grabbed the turkey and started stuffing him with almost violent gusto, humming carols to herself the whole time. When she came around to "Silent Night" in the Christmas jukebox in her head, it was always sung in German. Elizabeth noted her mother's unusual happiness, smiling to herself in a totally cheerful way, which Georgette had rarely allowed herself of late. Over the last few months worries had drained even the occasional smile from Georgette's lips and replaced it with a biting action on her lower lip that had Elizabeth concerned. But this morning her mother seemed almost bubbly.

Then standing in front of the kitchen window, Georgette's gaze left the half-filled cavern of the turkey and drifted out the window above the sink to the barn. The smiling and humming stopped and she bit her lower lip. Elizabeth watched her mother and picked up the bowls from the table. Some of the bowls that had contained the mush were empty and others were barely touched. The non-eaters hoped to last until something more to their liking was offered. Elizabeth took the bowls to the sink and stood next to her mother and followed her mother's gaze out to the barn. A shadow stood in the barn doorway; it was the shape of the only family member not in the kitchen, Raymond Sr.

Elizabeth waited respectfully for a few moments, then queried her mother, "Is he OK?"

"It is a terrible loss, dear."

"Will he be OK?"

Georgette's eyes filled with tears as she repeated to herself—would he be OK? This was a question that haunted her waking hours and dreams alike. Then considering the best answer for the children to hear, she became philosophical. "Time will tell," was her only reply.

At these awkward moments it seemed best to change the subject. With renewed enthusiasm, Georgette resumed the task of bird stuffing and sealed the filled cavern using a few deftly placed stitches made with a pair of wooden skewers.

"Now that that's done we have much more to accomplish," she announced to Elizabeth with a fresh dose of vigor.

The boys never really liked doing "women's work," as they called it. So in unison they sang out an appropriate "UGH!" Yet Georgette and Elizabeth knew that they would gladly help today. Tasty treats that were only seen once a year would be created today. That meant that there would be plenty of bowls to lick for the helpers. Sure they'd help.

Then without any prompting from the children, Georgette made official what they had already surmised. "We will be having visitors tonight."

Elizabeth winked at Justin who held up three fingers, one for each pie. Elizabeth and some of the brothers exchanged excited giggles at their deductive genius.

Then Justin remembered the most important visitor—well, at least on his list. "Yeah—Santa Claus!"

Georgette and Elizabeth shared a worried look.

"Yes, you could say that, Justin. Santa Claus will arrive tonight." Elizabeth gave her mom a quizzical look, then smiled knowingly, guessing at the real meaning of her mother's comment.

The boys painted cookies with white frosting and sprinkled them with various cookie decorations, but nearly in
unison they discarded the Santa bit and asked in earnest,
"No, Mother, who is coming?"

"Well…" She avoided a direct answer; it was more fun
to make a guessing game out of these rare visits. "Just
guess. Who could be a Santa to us?" Hands stopped frosting cookies as they pondered for a short while until Jeffery
tossed out the first guess.

"The landlord is giving us the place for Christmas." The
family frowned and with sarcastic chuckles of disbelief at
this ludicrous suggestion went right on with the tasks at
hand. Even full well knowing their plight, the accident and
all, the landlord hadn't knocked a dime off their rent payment once the harvest was in. In his defense Jeffery
snapped back, "Hey, it worked for the Cratchits, didn't it?"
His class had just read the Dickens's seasonal tale before
Christmas break, so the details were fresh.

Georgette laughed too heartily and Jeffery felt ashamed
and blushed, afraid that his answer had been in error somehow. "What, that old tightwad?" Georgette blurted out before she could catch it. She had said out loud a mean thing
in front of her children. Poor example of a mother, she said
to herself. Then quickly Doug shouted out his guess.

"Grandma and Grandpa?"

At hearing that as a possible guess, Georgette wrinkled
her brow so deeply you could have grown carrots in those
furrows. In fact, if she didn't relax that brow soon, she'd
have to dust it.

"When...(something inaudible to the children was mumbled here)...freezes over!" was her only comment. And Elizabeth could have sworn, if she was allowed to, that she heard her mother say "preacher words." Words that the preacher was allowed to read from the Bible or put in his sermons and prayers but words that resulted in a harsh smack to the face if they were ever uttered by a Huhn child.

Elizabeth remembered once when Doug had said "ass" at the supper table. It had been just after Palm Sunday. Upon hearing that one word, Raymond Sr. had pulled Doug from the table and smacked Doug's bottom half with the old belt that hung near the kitchen door. After a few hits Raymond Sr. asked his sobbing son, "Where did you hear such language?"

Through his sniveling, Doug tried to answer but couldn't, so Jeffery helped him out, "At church last Sunday."

Raymond Sr. reached out as if he were going to drag Jeffery off his chair. Raymond Sr. was at the ready, belt in his hand. He would give this insolent son a beating to match the one he'd just given Doug. Elizabeth could not stand to see any of her brothers hurt even when they deserved it, but this time it didn't seem fair, and she risked opening her mouth to protest, "Father, he did hear it in church."

"Georgette," Raymond Sr. yelled at his wife, "discipline that daughter!" This order usually meant that Elizabeth was slapped repeatedly. But as Elizabeth bent her head in horror of being slapped by her mother, she heard her mother argue with their father in front of the children in defense of the children, a very rare occurrence in this German family.

"Yes, Raymond, it was Palm Sunday and Jesus entered the city of Jerusalem seated on the colt of an ass."

Raymond Sr. unhanded Jeffery after little more than having tumbled the son from his chair. The father exited the kitchen, retreated to the back porch, very much stunned by it all, especially the fervor of his critique of his own child. He found himself mumbling a bit as he made his way from the porch to the barn where he went for solitude from his brood, "Yes, he did, and I agree he did," Raymond Sr. muttered to himself.

It was that incident, a year or two earlier, that had taught the children about "preacher words." Words the children knew were not to be uttered in the presence of adults in fear of a similar reaction. Yet the children knew that this was a double standard. Any adult could utter these words with little more than a raised eyebrow and nod toward the children.

But those memories were soon forgotten when Elizabeth yelled her guess of whom the guests might be, "I know who. I know. I do."

"Well, who, you silly goose? Quit squawkin' and tell us your guess." Doug was not in any way endeared to his older sister.

"It's Aunt Emily and Uncle Howard, isn't it?" She waited for confirmation but the smile on Georgette's face was sure to mean that Elizabeth had guessed it correctly.

"Yes, yes, I knew somebody would guess it."

The boys trumpeted gloriously at this confirmation. A celebration followed which included wads of cookie dough being gleefully flung at one another. While Georgette struggled to regain control, Raymond Sr. opened the door, taking one step into the kitchen. He witnessed behaviors from his progeny that he could not imagine his wife would ever tolerate. He turned around and retreated back out to the barn without saying a word, just shaking his head and mumbling something in German to himself. Justin had a wad of dough all ready to launch but took another look at it and popped it into his mouth.

The mayhem died down and Justin sought more information. "When will they be here?" he managed to articulate through the half-chewed wad of dough.

Georgette was giving stern looks to Jeffery who didn't seem to get the idea that the cookie dough fight would not be tolerated any more. She finally got his eye, and his cocked arm slowly dropped to his side and the cookie-dough-would-be-projectile was stuck back into the bowl. An action that raised hoots of disgust from all his siblings, "Ew."

"What?" he demanded.

No one gave him an answer—just more looks of disgust. "What!"

The other six ignored him. If he hadn't figured out that no one in the family had ever seen him voluntarily wash his hands, then none of them was going to explain it to him, at least not now. There were other topics to discuss, like the guests' arrival time.

"Well, Justin, the guests will show up when all the cooking and your chores are done and not a minute before."

With that announcement, the boys scrambled from the table, grabbed hats and coats without being told and ran out the door. A few of the boys even remembered not to let the door slam behind them. Elizabeth and Justin stayed behind to help Georgette finish the cooking. Clearing the remnants of the cookie battle would take some doing, Georgette thought, as she closed the door after the last of the exiting brood.

"Will wonders never cease? They have on coats and hats."

"They gotta be good, Mom, he's coming tonight."

Georgette gave a questioning look to Elizabeth.

"Who? What, Justin?" Justin answered sprightly and with disbelief that his own mom would need help with a topic so dear to his heart, "Santa Claus!" He glanced between Elizabeth and his mom trying to read their expressions. Was it really a hoax of some kind? "Santa is coming tonight!" He paused for recognition looks and then getting none, continued, "'Twas the night before Christmas…"

This time Georgette gave Elizabeth a worried look. How was it that she would have to disappoint such a faithful soul? But even the disbelievers Doug, Jeffery and Winston, who claimed they didn't believe in Santa, would still help put out cookies and milk every Christmas Eve before they went to bed, a treat that was to revive the weary traveler. They would even put out carrots for the reindeer if any were in the house that time of year. When Christmas Eve rolled around, these three were like deathbed converts.

In fact, the sun had hardly gone down and the boys demanded to be allowed to place the cookies and milk under the tree. Sadly, there were no carrots left in the root cellar this year, so they offered some pumpkin rind. "Heck, it's the same color—they won't notice. They're reindeer, for pity's sake," was Winston's rationalization. Then there was the argument about the cookies-and-milk placement. Some thought that it should be placed near the Franklin stove and others thought it best to leave it under the tree. The stove was the closest thing to a fireplace they had and it did have a chimney.

The debate ended with the family letting the smallest child decide, and Justin chose under the tree. "He's gonna be there placing the presents already. If we put it way over by the stove, he might not even see them."

Decision made, the plate sat expectantly under the tree next to Elizabeth's present. Jeffery poked at the cookies on the plate. Justin tapped Jeffery on the shoulder.

"Hey, Jeffery, if you don't believe in Santa, then who are the cookies for?"

"Just hedging my bets, m'boy, just hedging my bets." Betting wasn't allowed in this family, so Raymond and Georgette were giving one another looks like, "Now where'd he pick up that one?" Georgette just shrugged her shoulders and Raymond Sr. gave Jeffery an unexplained boot in the fanny.

"Hey," Jeffery started to protest then realized it was his dad, not a brother who had kicked him, and he quickly ignored the whole thing. He just rubbed the spot once with his hand and went on with his life.

Justin didn't understand what Jeffery's comment meant at all and looked to Elizabeth for help. "Wuzzat mean?"

"Nothing, Justin, and don't let them fool ya. They believe, all right." Georgette managed a smile as the headlights of their true Santas turned into the driveway.

Doug ran to the window to investigate. Headlights in their driveway were a novelty. "Look! They are here." Winston joined Doug at the window, both noses pressed to the glass and making smears on Georgette's clean windows.

"Well, it ain't no Ladies' Auxiliary this time," was Winston's full report.

Elizabeth joined them. "How do you know?"

Winston quickly replied, "'Cuz they turned up the drive like regular people."

"Yep, Mom, it's them," Elizabeth's voice rang with excitement. The children quickly left the window as the car occupants turned off the headlights and exited the vehicle. They all ran toward the kitchen because that was where the guests would enter and hand over their coats to Georgette.

Georgette was first to head into the kitchen to greet the guests while the children watched as packages started to emerge from the vehicle. Both Aunt Emily and Uncle Howard approached the kitchen door with arms overloaded with gifts. Justin was so excited over the appearance of the presents that he started hopping like a toad in springtime. He totally lost count of the packages, there were so many, and his eyes bugged out like the amphibian his hopping had imitated. "Yes, I do believe in Santa."

Justin finally stopped hopping and headed away from the window and followed the stream of brothers into the kitchen to greet the guests. He shouted to Elizabeth over his shoulder, "Look at what Santa gave them to deliver to us!"

"What?" Elizabeth wasn't following her little brother's train of thought.

"Santa! See what Santa gave them to deliver to us. It's a little early, but early beats none at all."

Catching his escaping hand she pulled him back toward her and whispered in his ear, "I told you that just having a stove wouldn't stop him. He'd find a way."

Each package that came into the house looked bigger and more fancifully dressed up in Christmas ribbons than the last. The brothers relayed packages from their aunt and uncle's arms to the place of honor under the tree. The adults were somehow able to ignore the children's bedlam on the floor as they hugged and shook hands with the usual adult greeting ritual.

Georgette's "Merry Christmas, you dear people" had her brown eyes brimming.

An armload of packages slid onto the floor from Aunt Emily's arms as she leaned over and let them tumble down. Standing upright, she stretched her arms out to all six happy children faces and boomed, "Merry Christmas to you all. And Happy Birthday to you, Georgette."

Then with great attention paid to watching Justin's face, she made the next declaration, "And there are more presents in the car." Justin's toad act reappeared. He hopped and bugged his eyes out and made a lap around the room like a whirling dervish. He could utter no words. The brothers were a bit more in control as they dashed out to the car with Aunt Emily leading the charge.

Uncle Howard came in with another armload, which he placed on the floor in a stack since the room under the tree was already taken by the first loads. As the brothers came back in the room, Uncle Howard gave his greeting to the children, "Merry Christmas and HO, HO, HO! All of these are directly from Santa. He asked us to deliver them. He was so busy this year, and frankly he wasn't too keen on all those potholes you have in this county."

Georgette broke in, "Oh, I do believe, Uncle Howard, that some of those potholes are heaven-sent." Howard gave his sister-in-law a smile with a quizzical look, yet neither one said anything more.

Elizabeth winked at Uncle Howard with a slight nod of her head toward Justin who was still hopping—at a lower frequency than before, but hopping just the same.

"He was running late again this year," Justin added knowingly.

"Exactly," replied Uncle Howard.

Justin's toad routine was finally interrupted when Georgette called them all to dinner, and Uncle Howard scooped him up and carried him into the kitchen, hugging him and tickling him the whole way.

Chapter 18

Good Grace

Dear Star,

Two main gifts have arrived, Uncle Howard and Aunt Emily. Now I must help Mom cook! You have never seen so many packages. The boys are beside themselves. I'd always wondered what that phrase meant until today—I have no doubts now.

Merriest of Christmases,

Elizabeth

All ten of them sat around the table as if it were King Arthur's court. A well-enjoyed meal was evidenced by the remnants that were scattered all over the huge kitchen table. The turkey was only half consumed. It had been described by one of the diners as being as large as a medium-sized dog. The children were all looking longingly at the living room where the tree held a bounty they'd never seen before. The tree lights reflected off their pupils gave the watching adults all the clues they needed to figure out where the children's thoughts were. Georgette began to clear the table, and rose looking to prove herself a grand hostess even if the surroundings were not matching her abundant spirit.

"Would anyone like anything more?"

The boys moaned in unison, "No." Which rewarded them a sharp look from both mother and father. Aunt Emily and Uncle Howard set the pace with the usual Christmas tease. For while the children would receive toys and new clothes and fancy candies, this once-a-year event, the adults were allowed to drag out the suspense for as long as possible.

"That was the tastiest turkey that I have ever had, Georgette. What did you do to get it that sweet? Willing to trade a secret or two?" Emily made small talk while she watched Doug's eyes roll back in his head from the boredom of this idle female chatter when there were gifts in the next room with his name on them.

"I just hope the one in the trunk of our car is every bit as tasty," added Uncle Howard in response to his wife's wink and head tilt toward the boys. Winston had just laid his head on his crossed arms on the table in front of himself. A nap would be better than to endure this adult torture.

"Oh, thank you so much! We can make a turkey last a long time around here and we do love 'em," Georgette added as she and Elizabeth scraped plates and piled them up to be washed—hopefully later, was Justin's thought. He eyed the huge stack of plates that Aunt Emily removed from the table. It would take hours to wash all those, he worried.

The children had locked their eyes on the booty under the tree and there was little chance that they were consciously following the adult gibberish enough to even understand that there were stall tactics going on by a deliberate group of adult relatives. Raymond Sr. winked at Georgette for the first time since the accident and joined in the adult pastime.

"So how about some of that pie, Georgette?"

Justin couldn't stand the thought of waiting for the adults to eat another course before he would get to unwrap a gift, and he blurted out his thoughts uncontrollably, "NO, don't eat dessert, too!"

His voice was so pleadingly sad that even Elizabeth came to his rescue.

"Can't we please have dessert after we unwrap presents?"

But then Raymond Sr.'s sadistic gene chimed in, "Who said anything about unwrapping presents tonight?"

Justin slumped into a position much like Winston had adopted earlier. Arms crossed on the table, he placed his head in this self-made cradle as the tortures continued.

Georgette now stepped in to do her part. "Christmas morning is a good time to unwrap gifts."

Justin's pile of parts moaned.

Emily couldn't stand it any longer—every child face was longer than a ride to a Christmas star. "Or..." She paused for effect, watching as Justin let one eye peer over his arm at her in hopes of a kinder verdict, "...we could unwrap tonight!"

Justin's head was birthed immediately from his arm cradle, and all the children cheered.

Georgette turned to stifle a laugh as she tried to seriously say, "But not until the dishes are washed."

The moans drowned out the adult laughter as the children's heads dropped back into their crossed arms.

Uncle Howard ended the torture and then became even more of a favorite uncle. "Enough of this teasing, I can't wait any longer! Let's unwrap now!" With that said, he jumped up from his seat, grabbed Justin from his chair, and led the parade into the living room. As if he were the Pied Piper, the children followed in an orderly fashion and sat on the floor close to the tree, waiting patiently for instructions on how to proceed from here.

The adults helped themselves to a cup of coffee. Emily poured two, one for Howard who was leading the distribution of gifts, having appointed Raymond Jr. to distribute them as the family "Santa." Present stacks were being made in front of each child. With the addition of each gift on their pile, the recipient's eyes widened. The other three adults entered the living room laughing, with coffee in hand, to find all six children behaving quiet as church mice.

Once all the gifts were distributed, the children looked around to get instructions from the adults. The adults looked around with little headshakes all in agreement, so Uncle Howard said, "OK, you can open now."

Never was there repeated in that small room a melee to rival the ripping and tearing that commenced. Having beautifully wrapped gifts for once in their life did not slow them down much.

To these children who were so used to hand-me-downs, even the gifts of clothing were very much appreciated. Each child had their very own set of gloves or mittens depending on their age, scarf, knit hat, socks, and unmentionables, too. The gloves and hats and scarves were immediately tried on and left on while they unwrapped the next gift. While wearing the new gloves did slow them down, they eventually realized this and the gloves were off again real soon. Once their fingers were released from the confines, they continued unwrapping with renewed swiftness. Along with the accessories, each boy received a new shirt, pair of pants, and sweater. It was clear that the clothes were very-much-appreciated new treasures in their lives.

Thank you's poured profusely from every corner of the room. Even though they were told that these treasures came from Santa, the thank you's went to Uncle Howard and Aunt Emily as the emissaries responsible for the delivery.

Then Uncle Howard tossed one more conspicuously shaped package to Raymond Jr. "You're the oldest, you do the honors."

Raymond Jr. looked around the room into each brother's face, for they all knew what it was. The brothers nodded wild encouragement, so without another hesitation, Raymond Jr. dug into the wrapping that poorly tried to disguise the gift of a football. There in his hands for the first time was his brand-new leather football. "Wow, that's the bee's knees!"

With an expert twirling toss into the air a few feet above his head and then safely catching the ball back in his hands, he asked, "Mom, can we go play?"

The four older brothers launched themselves from the living room floor in an instant. They trooped toward the kitchen door in their usual push-and-shove melee.

Georgette yelled in vain, "Coats! Hats!"

She shrugged at Raymond Sr. who looked his youngest in the eye and talked to him for what may have been the first time since the accident, "What, no football for you?"

"I'll watch Elizabeth unwrap," was Justin's meek reply. He'd seen what this man had done to his brothers in the past, so he just stayed around the ladies in the family. Hanging out with the older brothers could just mean that he would end up getting in on the group punishments that were meted out when his father didn't know whom to blame. Justin cuddled under Elizabeth's arm as she unwrapped. Justin was wearing every new thing that he had gotten including his new slippers. His new socks had been pulled onto his hands, which he was using as puppets. His own private puppet show was going on between his two hands.

Through the window behind the tree, the older boys could be seen throwing the football in the yard. Of course, they wore no coats or hats. Georgette just shrugged. "It hasn't killed any of them up 'til now."

The mound of presents in front of Elizabeth had every-one's attention. Aunt Emily couldn't stand it any longer. "So, dig in, honey."

Elizabeth's eyes danced as she looked at the huge box in front of her. The Ladies' Auxiliary box was still untouched under the tree, unnoticed now that so many rival gifts were there waiting to be discovered. Painstakingly, Elizabeth untied ribbons, unstuck tape, and gently lifted pieces apart so that she could save the paper. She folded each beautiful piece of wrapping paper lovingly before she even opened the box it had just graced. She sat the paper down next to her chair. Aunt Emily sidled her chair closer to Georgette and both ladies' hands were clasped tightly together, then Emily leaned in to whisper, "Thank you for letting me have the joy of giving to some children we dearly love this Christmas."

Georgette turned to look Emily in the eye and both women let the tears roll from behind the emotional dams that all good German stock learned to build early in life. But now with just family present, these two tough ladies allowed tear after tear to slide down a powdered cheek and onto their hands and laps. As Elizabeth parted the tissue that hid the enclosed gift from her view, she gasped and looked up to check to see if this box was truly hers.

Aunt Emily nodded. "Go ahead, it is yours, dear."

Georgette leaned in to whisper to Emily, "It's beautiful," as Elizabeth pulled the dress from the tissue. The first bit of blue velveteen was seen and then Elizabeth stood up, dress held in front of her as the box fell from her lap and hit the floor; she did a bit of a spin to show all just how lovely the dress was.

Words failed Georgette. "Oh Emily, Howard, it's…Thank you!"

Elizabeth squealed. A sound her mother had never heard her make before—a sound which so startled Georgette that she jumped a bit in her chair. Happy sounds from her children hadn't been heard for months. Georgette wondered if the children had been as scared as she had been at times, but just hadn't said anything. What could children have done or said that would have made any difference? So children suffer and worry in silence.

The dress was so lovely a possession that all Elizabeth could do to even approximate her appreciation was to circle the room, kissing and hugging each adult in turn, knowing somehow that this gift was a blessing from them all. Little did she realize that the biggest gift of all might have been the swallowed pride of her parents to even allow this bounty to befall them.

Uncle Howard accepted the affection and then pointed back at the pile of gifts. "There's more, dear," he said as he pointed to a three-foot stack of as-yet, -unwrapped packages. Howard then turned to his sister-in-law, "And a birthday present for you, Georgette." Georgette accepted the gift with a gracious no-words smile and nod, but laid the gift in her lap so she could first watch as Elizabeth unwrapped her bounty.

Elizabeth settled back in her chair to unwrap the tights, socks, gloves—and undies that caused her to blush and quickly put them back into the tissue. Occasionally the back door was heard to open and it was expected that a coat or hat was being garnered from the kitchen so that the football game could continue. When Elizabeth's stack of presents was unwrapped, the adults begged her to go try on her new clothes.

Aunt Emily looked at her watch then glanced toward Uncle Howard, "Well Elizabeth, why don't you go see how the dress fits?"

While in the lap of great abundance and in all the excitement, all the children had forgotten what had once been the only present in the house. The shoe box shaped present from the Ladies' Auxiliary had been inadvertently pushed back under the tree, hidden by the wrappings of the current bounty."

While Elizabeth was out of the room trying on her new clothes, Georgette and Emily conferred in serious whispers.

When Elizabeth finally made reentry, Aunt Emily and her mother had their hands clasped. Their tear-filled eyes revealed that the two ladies had made some solemn pact. All that was heard between the two ladies by Elizabeth was her mother saying, "I can't guarantee that she'll go. She gets so homesick."

Elizabeth heard those last words and painted a worried look on her young countenance but quickly twirled in her new dress and her smile returned. Justin reached up to touch the soft velveteen and was much impressed.

Uncle Howard spoke first, "Wow—such a princess."

A half-interested Raymond Sr. said, "Yeah."

Elizabeth gave a new round of hugs to everyone in the room with many thank you's, especially to Aunt Emily who finally admitted to sewing it herself. And when Justin gave his aunt a quizzical eye she added, "Santa requested the help. His elves get so tired."

Elizabeth didn't truly know how to possibly thank this couple who had taught her all she knew about the Christmas season's gift of giving. She knew what it meant to receive graciously when all hopes of receiving anything had been dashed long ago. So Elizabeth tried with one more utterance to say "thank you" when she knew that words would never be enough. "How can I ever repay you?"

A rhetorical question it may have been, but Aunt Emily took one last look from Georgette and found the courage to make her request. "I know something you could do."

Excited to repay her relatives, Elizabeth blurted, "What? Anything. What?"

"You could come with Uncle Howard and me to midnight church services and the family Christmas party tomorrow. We'll have you back here by bedtime tomorrow night."

Although her face did droop a bit at the first hearing of the proposal, she caught herself quickly, then looked to her mother.

Trying to convince herself as well as her daughter, Georgette agreed, "You are a big girl now—one night away from us…"

"Justin?" Elizabeth glanced at her now sleepy baby brother.

"He'll be just fine for one day."

Batting back a tear and hugging her mom, Elizabeth sealed the deal. "I'll go."

Aunt Emily jumped to hug her niece and then they quickly went into packing mode, for time was short.

"Should I take my dress off?"

"Oh, no, dear, you can leave it on. That way you will be ready for church at midnight—after a nap, of course."

Elizabeth stood still and reflected on the tree for a while. She soaked up what she feared would be the last bit of Christmas she would see that season. For when you have never traveled beyond your own backyard, you can only define your hopes and dreams on those limits. But for those who learn to leave the confines of their known world, great growth can begin. Dreams can then be seeded in a brand-new fertile spirit.

Chapter 19

When All You Had Was an Icebox

December 24,
Dear Star,

I won't have time to write much—the ladies think that I am trying on this lovely dress—but I also thought that I could journal about this beautiful dress. I can't believe my eyes when I look in the mirror. Everything is so splendid— soft blue velvet and red satin bows—so rich. I am the happiest that I have ever been. Now back to the living room before they miss me.

Love,

Elizabeth

Dear Star,

I can hardly write for the tears. Mom and Emily have
agreed that I go with Aunt Emily and Uncle Howard for the
night. Be away from Justin on Christmas Eve night and
Christmas Day? How could they even ask? How dreadful.
Mom said that I am old enough to spend a night away from
the family. But not this night. Oh, unfair. And I can't protest—it would hurt Aunt Emily so badly. So my fate is
sealed. My fate is not my own. I am but chattel to the
whims and wishes of the adults around me. I will be the
obedient daughter—Mom will be the one that has to bear
Justin's tears. That will be penalty enough for her decision.

More later,

Elizabeth

Georgette did the best she could. Feeding the children
had been a chore. She and Raymond were good farmers.
They timed the slaughtering so that little was wasted. Parts
were smoked, pickled, and canned, like the pig's feet. And
some were eaten right away, like the sweet sausages and
fresh pork tenderloins cut into medallions and served with
sauerkraut and candied yams. Then there were the pre-
serves, fruits to can, and tomato sauces to reduce and put
up. The piles of apples and potatoes would be nestled into
beds of straw in the root cellar to keep them from touching
and bruising. The straw would prevent many cases of rot by

winter's end. All those preparations were done without re-
frigeration. The icebox would keep the milk from spoiling
for a day or two and then they would have cottage cheese
for supper. But there was little else an icebox could do. It
was no wonder that these farm children had had very little
ice cream that wasn't hand-cranked on a summer's day
with ice and salt used to set the luxury hard enough to
scoop it up. This was experienced mostly at the church's
ice cream socials; the Huhn's didn't own an ice cream
maker. Nor had these country children had many of the
other foods that city folks took for granted. So part of the
evening that Aunt Emily had designed for Elizabeth was to
stop at a restaurant or two to introduce her niece to a vari-
ety of new food choices.

As Elizabeth rode along in the back seat of the 1939 car
still smelling strongly of that new car smell, she watched
the stars come out like fireworks against the Christmas sky.
Aunt Emily and Uncle Howard, however, were watching
the approaching car headlights with great interest. The
headlights seemed to be erratically jumping from one side
of the road to another. The aunt and uncle continued to
chatter about the brewing war in Europe. There was no
change in the tone of their voice so as not to alarm Elizabeth. Yet both of the adults knew that this oncoming car
was a threat to their safety. Emily glanced with furrowed
brow as she watched Howard and his reactions intently.
Howard slowed down considerably to make evasive action
easier on his part if it became necessary. Emily continued
to bounce her gaze from the errant car to Howard but said

nothing, as she trusted that he would make his usual good choices. He was a patient driver.

In a soft voice Howard finally commented on the car, "Looks like someone has had a bit too much Christmas cheer."

Elizabeth joined in the conversation. "How can you have too much of that?"

The two cars passed cautiously and Emily, Howard, and Elizabeth strained to see who was in the other car. Elizabeth recognized these two ladies with their mouths a' flapping as much as their fine winter hats that bounced feathers and fur trim with every shock of a pothole. It was Justin's two Sunday school teachers, the "delivery ladies" from the Ladies' Auxiliary.

The two ladies watched the passing car and saw Elizabeth. They waved wildly as did Elizabeth in return. Ida waved vigorously with a hand that would have been better used on the wheel but somehow the two cars passed without incident. Emma reached over to grab the wheel and waved at Elizabeth with her other hand, alternating between straightening her elaborate hat and the waving. The wheel hand switched between grabbing the wheel and attempting to steer and returning the slaps that Ida offered in response to Emma's grabbing the wheel. Both ladies' mouths never stopped moving. Their windows were partway down even in the cold, and the blaring Christmas carols pouring from their radio could be heard by the occupants of the other car as they passed.

Uncle Howard noticed Elizabeth's excited wave at these two curiosities and decided that he must know more. For

Howard found it odd that any folks that were in the inebriated condition that those two seemed to be in would ever come in contact with his teetotaling half brother's child. Even foods cooked with alcohol were not eaten or prepared by Georgette or anyone under her roof. "Do you know them, Elizabeth?"

"Yes," Elizabeth cheerfully answered. She quickly unbuttoned her coat and pushed the bodice of her new dress firmly against the car window in an attempt to have her new dress seen by these two friends. A glimpse of which put a huge smile on Aunt Emily's face. Too much time in a house full of brothers, was Emily's first thought. This visit would be so good for Elizabeth's budding womanhood. Elizabeth pulled her coat back together and buttoned it up as she turned to look out the back window. She knelt on the back seat, and continued waving at the now retreating Ford sedan. "It's the delivery ladies from the Ladies' Auxiliary from our church. They also teach Justin's Sunday school class. You should see the way they drive," Elizabeth laughed. "And the day they brought us a live turkey for Thanksgiving, the bird hated the potholes and pecked at them the whole time. By the time it got to our house, it was ready to die just as long as it got out of that car."

Howard added his comments, "Well, I can sure sympathize with the bird. They could use a few driving lessons."

Emily whispered to Howard, "And we thought it was Christmas cheer. Shame on us."

The '39 Ford in Howard's rearview mirror wasn't doing any better at managing the potholes, ice, and whatever other impairment might be working on the driver than they had been doing when they had approached him. He watched until they were out of sight to make sure that they didn't end up in a ditch.

The radio announcer had interrupted the Christmas carols to brief the listeners on the news of Hitler's latest advances. Then the carols started again and the peace of the starlit evening washed away the thoughts of war. As the three of them drifted into the wonder of yet another Christmas Eve, the jumbling of the car eventually rocked Elizabeth to sleep.

Uncle Howard's Studebaker pulled into the gravel driveway of a huge well-decorated house, complete with a Santa-and-sleigh arrangement in the front yard. A scalloped garland studded with white lights was fastened tastefully in place along the gutters with huge red velvet bows. Uncle Howard scooped Elizabeth into his arms and carried her into the house, up the stairs, into a bedroom, and laid her fully clothed on the pink lace-covered twin bed to allow her to continue her nap undisturbed. Howard pulled up a coverlet gently to her chin so as not to awaken her. Aunt Emily stood in the doorway watching this most wonderful Christmas dream come true. Reverently she placed her hand on her husband's back as he stood next to the bed alternating his own glimmering gaze between his wife's brimming eyes to the young lady asleep on the bed.

"Oh, I've dreamed of putting a little girl in this room for so long." The couple worked together to take off Elizabeth's old shoes, sat them on the floor next to the bed, and draped a heavier comforter over Elizabeth's still sleeping form. With the completion of those tasks, Aunt Emily clasped her hands together, looked to the ceiling, and mouthed the words, "Thank you." A prayer more heartfelt was rarely sent toward heaven. Uncle Howard stepped to his wife's side and slipped his hand into hers. Howard stooped to kiss Elizabeth gently on her cheek.

"Merry Christmas, dear sweet angel." The couple backed out of the room and softly closed the door behind them.

Rather than wear her old shoes to the church service, Elizabeth had convinced her aunt to let her wear a pair of Emily's low heels. "Just don't tell your mother!"

"I won't," promised Elizabeth who beamed back a big 'Thanks' to this sweet lady who seemed to understand her wish to grow up better than her own mother did.

There was a line just to enter the church. Since it was Christmas Eve, Aunt Emily had explained that arriving early was a must, "since some folks think that church attendance is a semi-annual event."

"What's that?" was the very question Uncle Howard had expected from his niece in response to his wife's remark. Howard lifted one brow in answer to Emily's facial plea for assistance.

"This one's all yours, dear," he replied to her unspoken request as they squeezed through the huge carved ten-foot-high double doors that had Elizabeth's attention diverted from her inquiry. The decorations in the church and the music of the organ had the youngster's mouth wide open in awe. She scanned the beautifully painted ceiling and en-sconced candles along the walls with that perfect tourist gape that one would expect from a farmer hitting the big city for the first time. A pew was found acceptable by the adults and they shuffled in first, allowing Elizabeth to occupy the aisle seat, affording her a better view. The hymnal was opened to the first carol and placed in her lap by Aunt Emily. Elizabeth sat, eyes closed and waited as patiently as she could through a prayer. She wanted so much to look more at the church and hear the organ. Very little delivery of the prayer could actually be heard anyway with its meaning so interrupted by the coughs and shuffling of the congregation. Elizabeth would open her eyes and peek to see if others were still "praying," had they lifted their heads yet, for not a word was working its way through her excitement. So when the first few cords of the anthem woke her from her pretended pious prayer, she jumped to attention, not expecting the force of the organ's voice.

The choir stood and started to sing Handel's "Hallelujah Chorus." Elizabeth rose with her aunt and uncle, keeping alive one more tradition of the season. It was clear that Elizabeth was enthralled with the sound so magnificent. She'd never heard this piece live before, only on the radio, which so dampened the forceful delivery of a live choir, that it was as if it was a first hearing. As the climax approached, Elizabeth strained to see over the heads of the adults as she hopped and shuffled to see more of the choir. Uncle Howard moved her into the aisle and stood there with her to satisfy her evidenced longing to see more. There from the aisle advantage she could see the faces of the singers that were filling the rafters with these celestial notes.

Aunt Emily, delighted by Elizabeth's enthusiasm, reached out for her hand and gave it a big squeeze accompanied with a smile to match. This was rewarded with a return in kind from Elizabeth. From that Christmas on, there would never be a musical performance that could match the "Hallelujah Chorus" for Elizabeth. The beams of joyous approval that gleamed in her eyes would testify that Handel and his music were life-long favorites from their first hearing.

The service over, the worshipers streamed out of the church doors. They walked to the car with Elizabeth bubbling her delight in what she had heard. "How can you describe such a sound? Why, the composer...who was he again?"

"Handel."

"Yes, Handel. Why, he must have been possessed."

"Possessed?"

"Yes, truly possessed of the Holy Spirit to have written such a song."

Uncle Howard and Aunt Emily smiled at her gleefulness and Howard affirmed her comments, "He surely must have been, dear."

The car circled through the town past all the factories that had set out elaborate holiday light displays. Nothing had ever been seen like this on the farm and Elizabeth absorbed it all with wonderment even though she was very tired.

Once home with her aunt and uncle, the dress was lovingly draped over the doorknob to wait for the Christmas party later that day, and Elizabeth snuggled into a new pair of pajamas with a matching robe. There was one more house tradition that she would later make part of her own family's Christmas traditions.

Aunt Emily had explained, "Well, before we go to bed on Christmas Eve at out home we are allowed to unwrap one gift."

"But Christmas is tomorrow." Elizabeth was worried that if she opened this gift, there might not be anything to open on the real day of presents.

Emily guessed her reluctance. "It's OK, Santa is bringing more tonight. You can open this one now."

Accepting the package in her lap with, "OK, I don't want to be accused of breaking any of your family traditions," Elizabeth ripped into the huge box that revealed a new coat and muff. Too fine for Tiffin, was the first thought that ran through her head. But she jumped up to try it on and demonstrated the perfect fit. A muff—wow, she'd always wanted one. Wouldn't the other girls be jealous? "Thank you, you are too generous."

"It is our pleasure. Now let's go brush those teeth and go to bed. We have to be up and headed to my family for the Christmas party in just a few hours."

Elizabeth's face fell a bit at the mention of the party. Along with being incurably plagued with homesickness, she was extremely bashful around strangers. The last thing she really wanted to do on Christmas Day was to spend it with a bunch of people she didn't know and who didn't know her.

Tucked in, prayers said, Uncle Howard read her "The Night before Christmas." Her aunt and uncle kissed her forehead, turned out the lights, closed the door, and left her alone to sleep.

Alone was a most unfamiliar state. Such a rarity that she wasn't sure she wanted to become accustomed to it. Unable to sleep, she looked out at the stars as they danced behind a thin lacy cloud curtain. She realized it was probably the very same star Justin was watching from his bedroom window, all alone with no big sister in the room to comfort him for the first time since he was born. Somehow she felt like she had deserted the little fellow, and begged the star to take care of him and comfort him in her absence. The star twinkled back at her. Justin had told her the twinkle meant the star had received the request and you would get your wish. With that as her comfort, Elizabeth finally went to sleep.

Not long after Elizabeth had left with her aunt and uncle, Justin discovered the unwrapped present from the Ladies' Auxiliary still under the tree. He retrieved the package and carried it into the kitchen to show his mother. As a tear slid down his cheek he held up the present, "She didn't unwrap it," he managed to get out between the sobs.

"Oh my," Georgette sighed as she scooped both Justin and the present into her arms, "We'll make sure that it is the first thing she does when she comes home tomorrow night, honey. OK?"

Justin shook his head to the affirmative and allowed his mother to rock him before he went to bed. She read him the "Night Before Christmas" while pointing to each word as he followed along.

Justin was curled in his featherbed nest, cuddling his much-loved sock lamb that Elizabeth had made him. A tear rolled from his eye to dampen a streak on his cheek and left a small wet spot on his pillow. But before another tear could be produced, his star twinkled and winked at him. He turned toward the window to watch it better and it winked again, just for him. He was sure. The little brother knew Elizabeth was watching the same star and he fell asleep praying that the star would keep his sister from being too homesick. All night his guardian angel stood next to his sleeping head to comfort him. One more gift Elizabeth had sent to her little brother, someone to watch over him in her absence. The angel vanished once Justin awakened on Christmas morning.

The next morning was all craziness trying to get ready and out of the house, "and this was only three people," Elizabeth whispered to herself. But in this family there were so many more details to attend to than at home. She had twice as many articles of clothing that were required and each had to be in perfect condition or much fuss was made. Aunt Emily was putting a few more bows on some presents and Uncle Howard was cramming the car full of presents. After Aunt Emily had finished wrapping each new present, it was Elizabeth's job to place the packages at the back door to make it easy for Uncle Howard to quickly load the car. Again she was allowed to wear a pair of her aunt's shoes. She felt like such a lady. Granted she was a bit wobbly at times but she was quickly mastering her new heights.

Juice and a cinnamon roll would have to hold them until they could stop along the way for a snack, was the promised agenda from Aunt Emily. Elizabeth had packed the new sleepwear neatly in a brown paper bag that was her luggage and she had slipped on the new dress. Who was that girl in the entryway mirror in a new coat and muff? The packed brown bag in her hand reassured her that tonight she would be back with Justin again. She worked to convince herself that the day of partying with Emily's relatives would be fun and tried to be cheerful without her family on Christmas Day. What had she agreed to?

As they left the house, Elizabeth marveled at the presents everywhere in the car and especially the flat rectangle box that was tied to the roof of the car. These people must be terribly wealthy, for such generosity was never before imagined in her old world.

After driving for about an hour they were all terribly hungry and Uncle Howard found a small café alongside the road that was open on Christmas Day. As he pulled the car into a spot right next to the front door, always the perfect host, he invited them to breakfast.

"How's this, ladies? We'll have breakfast here so we won't show up at your mother's house starving and demanding to be fed immediately."

"An excellent idea," Emily agreed.

Aunt Emily turned to check with Elizabeth in the back seat. "And for you?"

Elizabeth nodded eagerly, making it unanimous.

The restaurant was ablaze with tacky old Christmas decorations, too many of them from too many Christmases ago. The desserts were held in a refrigerated revolving display that immediately held Elizabeth's attention. All the desserts looked so fresh and there were so many choices. Elizabeth approached the display and watched as the parfaits, cakes, pies, and dishes of Jell-O whirled by.

As they were seated and handed a menu, Aunt Emily helped Elizabeth off with her coat and offered, "You can have anything you want, dear, anything at all."

Elizabeth had been reading the menu but looked up to make sure she had heard correctly. "Anything?"

"Yes, anything."

Her eyes locked onto the spinning dessert display and she knew what she wanted. She pointed at the case and told her uncle, "That's what I'll have, please."

Aunt Emily clarified, "A cheesecake for breakfast?"

"If that's what she's hungry for…" Howard chastised his wife.

Elizabeth corrected her order, "No, I want the Jell-O, just the Jell-O, please."

Aunt Emily and Uncle Howard exchanged amused smiles. "OK, and what flavor would you like, m'lady?"

Cautiously, Elizabeth answered, "One of each, please?"

With great aplomb, Uncle Howard grandly ordered for his ladies. Snapping his fingers in the air with great feigned importance and mock pretension, he called the waiter/owner as if summoning a maître d' in a fine restaurant, "Sir, service, please."

The restaurant owner had a sense of humor and came over to the table all caught up in Uncle Howard's theatrics; as the ladies giggled their delight at such attention, the owner snapped a towel from his apron string and draped it over his arm.

He bowed a greeting to the table and replied, "Why yes, monsieur. Vat vil it be?" His pretend French accent brought more giggles from the ladies.

With a flourish, Uncle Howard ordered for them, "We'd like Jell-O for the princess, please." And then under his breath a bit he added, "And please make that one of each flavor, sir."

"Why of course, monsieur."

There weren't many things that had been impossible with just an icebox, but Jell-O was one of them. Here was one treat that Elizabeth had seen in the grocery stores but it had not passed her lips very often. Occasionally a church potluck would have some Jell-O make an appearance, but it was such a treat to the farm children that there was rarely any left by the time she would get through the food line. So here on Christmas Day, she finally got her fill of Jell-O for the first time.

The restaurant owner, towel still draped over his arm, watched with Uncle Howard and Aunt Emily as Elizabeth gleaned the last morsels of lime Jell-O from the last dish. With great relish she stacked the empty dish on top of four other empty dishes to declare, "My, that was wonderful."

Uncle Howard, delighted with her contented smiling face, offered, "You sure you don't want more?"

"No, really. I'm full, thanks."

As the owner smiled and cleared away the plates and empty dishes, Uncle Howard inquired, "So what flavor is your favorite?"

"Oh, the lime, by all means. The lime is superior in every way."

"Now we have a Jell-O connoisseur in our midst," Uncle Howard added. He and Aunt Emily chuckled together as they donned their coats to leave.

Chapter 20

The Bargain

December 25, 1939
Christmas Day
Dear Star,

I am writing in the back seat of the car. I'm with Aunt Emily and Uncle Howard as we head to her family's Christmas party. I am dressed like never before in my life. A new dress still fresh even though I did wear it to the Christmas Eve services last night.

Wow, how to describe that experience? The church was huge. The sound of the organ and the choir together was, I believe, strong enough to lift the rafters right off the roof. I'm sure the glory that the sound gave to God was well received on high as it was by me here on earth. A piece of

Handel's *Messiah* was the music they played. The "Hallelujah Chorus," it was indescribable.

Singing along to the Christmas carols that were accompanied with full organ and choir was such a treat. Worth abandoning Justin on Christmas Eve? Probably not, but then it wasn't my decision. So I'm just enjoying it so far.
Well, we are just about to the party. Not really looking forward to this either. I tend to feel like a duck out of water around strangers. Especially when I know I will be a little farm kid surrounded by big city people. I'll try to be a big girl about this though. Wearing high heels makes me feel like I can handle this party like an adult, not a little kid.

Christmas wishes,

Elizabeth

The entry into the Christmas party would scare any wall-flower right into the wallpaper and of course the noise of children made crazy with Christmas anticipation, the loud chatter of eggnog-loosened conversation from the adults, and just the size of the house alone did all work to overpower Elizabeth and into the wallpaper she went. Her coat was taken off and placed with her muff somewhere in a far-off room. She was captive now, while Aunt Emily and Uncle Howard, assisted by other nieces and nephews, worked to unload the gifts from the car and place them under the enormous tree. Emily had guessed that the tree was twelve feet tall. Elizabeth sidled up to the tree to inspect the ornaments and gasped at the drenching of evergreen and red bows and white lights that the room had received in anticipation of this day, this event.

Each ornament would have been dear enough to pay for her family's whole collection of ornaments. There were blown Bavarian glass ornaments, hand-painted wonders with almost a gaudy appearance. But she marveled at them all then found a chair by the fire, embarrassed to be left on her own with strangers but finding some relief in staring at the fire. There had been some presents under the tree when she had arrived, but now they had occupied most of the floor space within five feet of the lowest branches of the tree. This flooding of gifts at the base of the tree was caused mainly by the additional gifts brought in by Aunt Emily and Uncle Howard. Good thing she had studied the ornaments earlier, she mused. She could not get close enough to the tree to do so now due to the quantity of presents.

But then another car pulled up outside and the gifts that they brought in made it necessary to stack them at least two feet high in order to make space for people in the room. Along with the gifts in the last car to arrive, a quite handsome young man about her age had also been delivered. Perhaps he was a little older. As he entered, Aunt Emily and Uncle Howard pointed him toward Elizabeth and he smiled and carefully nodded and replied to whatever instructions they gave him. During their conversation he glanced back to watch Elizabeth intermittently. Each time he caught her looking back, she stared at her hands in her lap or at the fire, embarrassed that he was looking so often in her direction.

Elizabeth watched as he walked directly toward her. She knew that she must have been blushing because her cheeks were hot even before she turned her head in the direction of the fire. She was confused as to the proper way to behave. But Greg was ready to ease her apprehension with a big smile and warm handshake.

"Hello, Elizabeth."

"Hello," she almost whispered in reply.

"My name is Greg. I'm a nephew of your aunt Emily. Welcome to my grandmother's home."

"Thank you." Her cheeks burned again so she turned her head back to the fire.

"Nice fire."

"Yes, it is." Followed by an uncomfortable silence until Greg quickly covered it over.

"Usually there is a jigsaw puzzle sitting out somewhere for us grandchildren to work on. Would you like to help me find it and work on it?"

"Sure...yes, I'd like that." The only jigsaw puzzles in her family were missing a few pieces or were Justin's and were just too easy to hold her interest. This one was found in the den, laid out on a mahogany table in a mahogany room. The room was lit with candles and a fire of its own. The room was graced with a tree and Christmas greenery enough to have been the main attraction in most homes. Yet in this house it was just a scaled down version of the master tree in the great parlor.

Greg inspected the work done by others. "Hum, looks like they are stuck on a piece with blueberry pie in one corner and part of a candle in the other." He checked with Elizabeth, "Think we can find it?" Elizabeth nodded and they both set to looking through the pieces.

Together they nearly finished the puzzle with lively conversation from Greg that had Elizabeth totally at ease.

A bell was rung by one of the adults in the parlor and the whole extended family knew to flock back to that room to grab a seat by the tree. Upon first hearing the toll of the bell, Elizabeth did nothing. Yet Greg dropped the puzzle pieces that he had in his hand and grabbed Elizabeth's hand instead. He led her at a trot back to the parlor while explaining their urgency to her over his shoulder.

"Come. Its unwrapping time." Greg hopped once as he cleared the threshold of the den, pulled her down the hall with great laughter, and they broke into the grand parlor at the same time as most of the other guests. The little ones had already found spots on the floor nearest the tree and sat cross-legged right up against the avalanche of packages. They giggled and poked one another to release some of the adrenaline of the moment. All of the little ones had at least one package in their laps already, which just wound them up to an even higher frequency of anticipation.

Elizabeth remembered her brothers' behavior of the day before and smiled fondly at these little ones. Aunt Emily's father took the role of Santa Claus the ringmaster, looking at the tags and calling out names. The room hushed to allow the caller to be easily heard and thus the footfalls of the package retrievers echoed in the almost silence.

"Here's one for Greg," said his grandfather, "and while you are here, take this one back to Elizabeth."

Elizabeth heard her name and was stunned that a gift was there for her. Greg had to coax her to accept the gift upon his return.

"For me?"

Greg obliged her and looked at the tag and nodded his head enthusiastically in the affirmative.

"But who?"

Greg took the tag in his hand again and read it for her, "From Mom and Dad and me."

He smiled at her unexpectancy and she finally smiled back.

"Thank you...but I didn't..."

Greg quickly anticipated the direction of her remark and interrupted.

"It's not the getting in return that makes giving fun. Let us have the pleasure of giving without the expectation of return, please."

Elizabeth's name was called again. She was waved toward the tree to retrieve the gift herself this time by Greg and others. She maturely walked up to gain yet another gift. During the gift dispersal she ended up with seven sweetly wrapped gifts in her lap. More gifts than she had remembered in one season ever had already been bestowed on her, and now this. Her perceived great bounty still looked scarce in comparison to the stacks of gifts in front of the other children. As the unwrapping began she discovered treasures from people she didn't even know. One gift contained a rhinestone bracelet, which elicited all the expected oohs and ahhs from her, much to Greg's pleasure. She checked the names on the gift tag and quickly committed them to memory. Next she opened a small porcelain box with velvet lining in which to place the most precious trinkets—like the bracelet, she quickly decided. She also received a lace hanky, a lovely silk scarf, mittens with rabbit fur lining, and a small bottle of lemon-verbena toilet water. She watched the rest of the unwrapping frenzy, and when all the loot seemed to have been uncovered and thank you hugs were delivered with squeals of excitement from the recipients of the most-wished-for items, Uncle Howard acknowledged a nod from Aunt Emily's father and the two men left the parlor together. Upon their return they had a huge rectangular box displaying a huge red ribbon, the box balanced between them.

The room started to buzz. Who might that big gift be for? Greg leaned over to Elizabeth all hopeful, "Big enough for a bike?"

Elizabeth nodded in agreement and Greg got noticeably more excited. She sensed his anticipation and crossed her fingers, looked to the sky, and closed her eyes for the briefest of prayers.

The big box that had been on the top of Uncle Howard's car earlier this morning was now in position in front of a now present-less tree, Uncle Howard fumbled with the tag for added drama. He finally gave up his attempt to read the tag and handed it over to Aunt Emily's father.

"Here, Dad, you do the honors."

New Shoes for Elizabeth

Emily's father, who was, of course, Greg's granddad, puffed his chest out as if he were reading a king's proclamation, and announced in his most official-sounding theatrical voice, "'Merry Christmas from Grandma, Grandpa, Mom and Dad. Much love to you.' Greg. This present seems to be yours, Greg. Come up here and claim it."

Greg didn't take more than a few steps and a hop to show his excitement as he scooted across the floor saying repeatedly under his breath nervously, "Right, so right."

Greg tore into the box and soon, with some help from his uncle and granddad, was able to pull the most beautiful black, thin-wheeled English bicycle into view. There were muffled gasps from the other children in the room. This was the most beautiful bike that Elizabeth had ever seen. Greg ran over to his mom, dad, and each grandparent to thank them with a big hug and kiss even before he sat on the seat. He repeatedly said thanks and "Wow, a Dawes three-speed—wow!"

As he put one foot on a pedal, Grandmother tilted her head toward Granddad and he whispered in Greg's ear. The other children crept toward him slowly as if in a revered state and then began begging riding requests before Greg could get three feet away. Greg's father stepped in to set down some rules.

"Well take it outside to ride it for starters; do let Greg get one good ride on it, and then take turns trying it out."

Elizabeth walked over and stroked the chrome handlebar and looked Greg right in the eyes. His facebeaming.

"It is so beautiful."

Greg nodded in agreement. "So come ride my bike with me. You can have the second turn right after my inaugural ride."

Some other child thought that he had the rights to the second ride somehow and lodged a protest that Greg quickly stared down.

"No, that's OK. I'll stay here where it's warm. Thanks." Elizabeth gladly declined a trip into the sunny but bitter cold Christmas Day.

Greg didn't argue and rolled right on down the hall, turning into the kitchen and out the back door, riding down the three shallow steps without once leaving the seat. He was followed by a gaggle of honking cousins. Elizabeth watched from the window by the tree as the children did manage to take orderly turns. The other adult relatives watched from a closer window. Aunt Emily was concerned over Elizabeth's solitude. She joined Elizabeth with an offering of hot cider and sat in the window seat next her.

"You OK, Sweetie?"

"Just fine. Your relatives are so kind and generous."

"Yes, they are. I think I'll keep them." The comment didn't get the expected chuckle Aunt Emily had hoped for. She watched Elizabeth closely and saw that her gaze was fixated on something. Clueless to figure out what had her niece's rapt attention, she rambled on, "So, what do you think of Greg?" What was Elizabeth supposed to say in reply? So Elizabeth said exactly what was true in this case, even though the words would have been the same even if it hadn't been the truth. Her mother had taught her some manners.

"He's so dear." She got the words out in spite of the temperature of her cheeks.

Aunt Emily sipped her cider and so did Elizabeth. Something is on her mind, is all the aunt could think about. Was she homesick and about to break into tears any minute?

"Why don't you go out and play with the others?"

"Really, thanks, but it is too cold for my liking. The fire feels much better."

Aunt Emily decided to leave her niece to her thoughts. Everyone needs to be alone with their thoughts sometime during the day.

Emily placed her hand on Elizabeth's shoulder. "You let me know if you need anything."

Elizabeth sipped her cider still transfixed on something out in the yard that her aunt and uncle determined to decipher. These two were plotting something. Emily approached Howard and they exchanged a few moments of whispering.

"Doesn't she want to go out?"

"She says that it's too cold. Poor thing is best by the fire. She has not one ounce of fat on her."

Emily watched from a distance as the cousins dragged an older bike from the barn, Greg's old bike. It was still a nice bike. All the pieces were there but it wasn't all shiny like the new bike. None of the children were seriously riding the old bike. It couldn't compete with the seductive black and mirrored chrome of the gift bike. Elizabeth, however, didn't take her eyes off the old bike. Uncle Howard watched her long enough that he thought he knew what she was watching, and he whispered his theory to Emily. Emily nodded with beaming eyes in agreement to Howard's proposal. The two locked hands and walked over to Elizabeth's spot in the window seat. They conferred as they closed the distance between themselves and their niece.

"One week?"

"I'll try for that."

Howard stopped to pull a chair up next to the window seat, as Emily sat herself next to Elizabeth. Once they were all on the same level and Emily had reached out to hold one of his hands and one of Elizabeth's, Howard started to talk. There was no doubt in his mind that his niece had been looking at that old bike the whole time.

"It's a shame that nobody wants that old bike."

Elizabeth took the bait and snapped to attention, "Oh, that's not so at all!" She exclaimed a bit too energetically for a mannered lady, she thought, and gained control a little better.

"Why, Elizabeth, would you like that old bike?"

Her answer surprised him. "No, not really."

Both aunt and uncle had a cloud of disappointment cover their faces. Then Elizabeth finished her thought, "But my brothers would kill to have it."

Enhanced glances confirmed that the aunt and uncle should go with their original plan. Emily nodded for Howard to go forward.

"Well, Aunt Emily and I have a way for your brothers to have that bike."

"Anything!" was Elizabeth's soon-to-be-regretted instant reply.

"We'd hoped that you would feel that way," replied Emily.

But Elizabeth's tone became mildly cautious. "Why? What do you want in return?"

"We'd like you to spend the next week with us."

Elizabeth's first thought was that they had broken their promise, but on second thought she realized that this was a whole new deal in the making. So she began to make the bargain.

"You promised that I'd go home tonight."

"We will honor our promise. We will take you and the bike home to your brothers tonight if you will stay with us one week."

As Elizabeth hesitated just a bit longer than Uncle Howard had hoped, he modified the deal, "Really only five days. We'll have you home a couple days before New Year's."

Elizabeth looked at the old bike one last time. "And all the Jell-O I want all week long?"

The adults glanced at each other once for solidarity and nodded their agreement.

"Well," thought Elizabeth, "it is a far better thing that I do…"

"What, dear?"

Elizabeth decided that Dickens was probably appropriate, just not that book, and she simply answered, "Yes, I'll do it."

Before the message that she had just spoken reached her brain and she could worry about being homesick for five days, a squealingly happy Aunt Emily was hugging her.

Realization set in and Elizabeth looked a bit sad about her hasty decision.

Uncle Howard reassured her, "You have just granted us our Christmas wish and your brothers', as well. How does it feel to play Santa Claus for seven people?"

Elizabeth's solemn face started to brighten. "You know, that feels pretty good."

Uncle Howard and Aunt Emily continued to hug her and she continued to smile through all that emotional attention as her teary eyes were still fixed on the old bike. Her brothers were getting a bike for Christmas.

"Wait 'til my brothers see this!"

Chapter 21

Post-Christmas Santas

December 25, 1939
Late Evening

Dear Star,

I have struck one more deal. I agreed to spend five days with Aunt Emily and Uncle Howard, if they would give my brothers Greg's old bike. It felt good to be a Santa at the age of thirteen and give my brothers the very gift I knew that they wanted down to their very souls.

I never dreamed that I could give to others when I had no money. Aunt Emily said gifts of the heart happen as if they were miracles, because we are thinking of others above ourselves. One thing is for sure, I love the feeling that giving can give me. Not only did I give to my brothers but I also have given five days to Aunt Emily and Uncle Howard. The only person not getting a good dose of holiday cheer out of this is Justin. But Mom has promised to bake cookies with him every day and that has quieted him down some.

He did shed a tear as I explained that I'd be gone for five more days. Hopefully he'll forgive me someday for this first desertion. Mom says as I get older that I will be doing more things away from the family. This is just the first of many adventures I'm sure.

Now I must stop writing and pack.

May all your Christmas wishes come true,

Elizabeth

As her brothers frolicked in the barnyard on their "new" bike, Justin sat pouting on Elizabeth's bed, watching her pack for five days away from home, as if one night of separation from her hadn't been hard enough. Elizabeth tried to be chipper while she packed, for Justin's sake. If he thought she was really excited to go, he'd deal with the issue better, just because he loved her so much that he didn't want her to be disappointed.

Somehow the idea that she could give her brothers a present so huge for nothing still amazed her. She was caught up in the whole idea of being able to give, not just receive. She was really just a kid herself, but look at those crazy brothers fighting over THEIR bike. And she did that. Maybe it's not what's in your pocket that counts at Christmas. In the long run, it's what's in your heart that matters most.

Another squeeze from Justin and she was in the back seat of the car facing backward, kneeling on the seat, as Jeffery tried to keep up with the departing car on the bike. Uncle Howard drove down and out of the Huhn family driveway. Elizabeth waved feverishly at Justin who stood on the porch next to Georgette waving good-bye to the vanishing car. Winston was on the back fender of the bike. Jeffery peddled feverishly yet was losing ground in the race with the Studebaker. Jeffery decided to lighten his load a bit in an effort to win the race with the departing auto. He solved that issue quickly. He simply reached back and knocked Winston off the back fender and into the brown slush that was the driveway. This allowed Jeffery to almost close the gap as the car slowed to turn onto the county road. Jeffery threw Elizabeth a kiss, the first time she ever remembered her brother showing her any affection at all. Uncle Howard gently pressed the accelerator and the race was over. Elizabeth turned around to face forward on the back seat and smiled. She closed her eyes and replayed the scene of Jeffery blowing her a kiss from the "new" bike. She smiled again as a tear slid down her cheek.

Justin had left the porch and disappeared into the house. He quickly reappeared. He had the Ladies' Auxiliary package in his hand and he was waving it frantically over his head. He was jumping up and down doing his toad impression again in hopes that the increased energy would get their attention. If energy could make up for his small size he had pulled it off, but no one in the car could see him or what he was doing. They had rounded the corner at the end of the drive already. Georgette consoled her now crying youngest, as best she could. The package was again placed under the tree to await Elizabeth's return. Georgette and Justin baked the first batch of cookies as she had promised him. In fact, Justin was pampered by the whole family, for the entire five days. He was allowed many more cookies than usual and Georgette read stories every few hours. Even the older boys toned down their tortures during the absence of Justin's favorite family member. Georgette even made a batch of her wonderfully smooth chocolate fudge, a real favorite of Justin's.

Foe Elizabeth, there were no tears for entire visit with he aunt and uncle.. Those five days were like an exquisite vacation and education for Elizabeth. She ate Jell-O at least twice a day, much to the delight of her aunt and uncle. Aunt Emily took Elizabeth shopping almost every day, which taught her a whole lot of lessons in living and surviving in the big city.

Upon entering Tideky's department store, Elizabeth saw her Christmas dress in the window and stopped to admire it. Aunt Emily stopped with her. "So?"

"You did a super job. Mine looks every bit as store-bought as that one."

Hand in hand they finished the walk to the store entrance, taking it ever so slowly so Elizabeth could catch every detail of the holiday window displays. Aunt Emily dropped Elizabeth's hand as they approached the revolving door. They let a few folks go through so that Elizabeth could observe how this was maneuvered. Folks jumped into a compartment and they twirled a bit and disappeared into the store. It looked simple enough.

"Ready?"

"Sure."

Yet when Aunt Emily slipped skillfully into a revolving door compartment, Elizabeth jumped into the same compartment with her. After much stumbling, bumbling, and laughter, they tumbled into the store. Aunt Emily brushed her coat off. "Well, that went well."

Elizabeth, still laughing, exclaimed, "Next time I bet I'm supposed to get in my own space, right?" In spite of some disapproving salesclerks at the perfume counter, everyone else seemed to comprehend the situation and enjoyed a chuckle and laughed with these two gleeful female shoppers.

"It is a proven fact, dear. One person per compartment works much better." They clutched hands and attacked the first floor, after trying on some imported French high heels with four-inch spiked heels.

Of course Aunt Emily had to hang on to Elizabeth for this to even be a possibility. Elizabeth admitted, "Mom might not approve of this."

"I'll take full responsibility."

Elizabeth glanced at the price tag as she placed her aunt's sensible shoes on her feet again. "Why, you could buy a good used car for that!"

"Yes, you could," remarked Emily. "But some people do have that kind of money."

They tried on shoes for over an hour. The pair that Elizabeth liked the most was not available in her size. Her aunt reassured her that they could order the correct size and in a couple of weeks the shoes would show up in the mail. Elizabeth agreed to this readily. The delay would be worth it. This pair of shoes would be the envy of every thirteen-year old girl in Tiffin. Her aunt made the arrangements with the salesman and their shopping spree continued.

"OK, now let's go get you a school outfit. Girls' clothes are on the third floor."

They reached the escalator and Emily grabbed Elizabeth's elbow and literally lifted her onto the contraption. Elizabeth became weak kneed and her aunt's hand firmed its grip on Elizabeth's arm. Elizabeth finished her escalator-ride debut successfully.

"Well, that went better than the revolving doors," Elizabeth proudly offered. Aunt Emily smiled as Elizabeth went to look at a counter of goods, still evidently a bit on the fainty side.

Her aunt went over to her side. "We have another flight to go. Or we could use the elevator."

"No, let me master one mechanical wonder at a time, please."

By the end of the day, Elizabeth was an escalator pro. No hand-holding was needed any more. The packages kept mounting. Every department seemed to hold something that Elizabeth "couldn't live without," according to Aunt Emily.

The five days flew by. It was time to go back to her brothers. Back home, she hoped that her brothers would ride the bike out to greet her. Yet even as the car grew closer, there was still no bicycle greeting party. Elizabeth worried that they had taken it apart and couldn't get it back together again, something that they did with many items around the farm. But as she hugged Justin first, then her mom and dad, and then each brother let her hug them, too, she gathered the information bit from one brother by another bit from another brother, until she and the aunt and uncle knew what had happened in only five days to that bike. Really, they'd hit a nail and flattened a tire two days after Christmas.

Uncle Howard was quick to take action. He loaded the four older boys into the car, strapped the bike onto the back, and drove into Tiffin looking for the hardware store.

Meanwhile the ladies and Justin helped Elizabeth unpack. Raymond Sr. wandered back out to the barn, alone again.

At the hardware store, the flat was repaired and the boys cheerfully wheeled the bike out. Uncle Howard stayed back in the store to strike a deal with the shop owner. Howard paid four times the price that was raised on the cash register.

"Fix it for them whenever it breaks, please. Next time I'm in town, let me know what else I might owe you."

"Understood."

On the car ride home, Jeffery was worried. "Thanks for fixin' the flat, Uncle Howard."

"Hey, don't worry about it. That's the least I can do for you boys for loaning us your sister all that time."

"Hey, take her back with ya again tonight if ya got anything good to trade," Doug offered.

Uncle Howard chortled his reply, "What would Justin say about that?"

"So take that little pip-squeak, too," added Winston.

"And what might your mom and dad say to that?"

"Well, Mom might say somethin' but Dad doesn't say much at all anymore," Raymond Jr., the usually quiet one, informed.

"But what if we get another flat?" Doug worried.

"Don't worry about it ever again. I made a deal with the hardware shop owner. For the price of that one tire, your bike is guaranteed for life. You take it in there and he'll give you the parts to fix it."

"Wow, that's some guarantee," Jeffery piped in.

The rest of the ride home they just listened to the world pass as only the male species seems to do contentedly.

As Elizabeth unpacked her new little suitcase—a satchel, Aunt Emily had called it—Justin cuddled her flannel pj's. Aunt Emily laughed at him, "Would you like some of your own?"

Justin jumped up onto the bed and started his toad dance again. "Yes," he croaked.

"Somehow I thought so." Emily tossed him another Christmas package and he dug into the box to uncover his very own soft flannel pj's. A squeal from him showed that these pj's were a hit as he scrambled off to probably put them on.

"It's like Christmas all over again," he shouted as he dashed away.

When the boys returned from town, there were more gifts for each of them. Every boy had a pair of waterproof rubber boots and some shirts. A huge roll of cash was placed in Raymond Sr.'s good hand as Howard whispered to him. "That's what brothers are for. And don't you ever forget it again."

"Half brothers," Raymond Sr. even chuckled a bit as he said it. "Let's just say we each got the good half."

For the first time in their adult lives, these two brothers hugged and laughed. Raymond Sr. had hesitated at this hug stuff, for he had always been uncomfortable with displays of affection. Yet his daughter was hugging even her brothers. The boys, like their father, were having some trouble with this new wave of affection, but they adapted. As she hugged her mom and dad, Elizabeth mouthed the words "missed you." The long days away were over. She was back home, however humble it was. She was home, back in a community that cared for its own, one that continued to feed them through the long winter ahead.

When all the new presents were unwrapped, Raymond SR. went to the barn and brought out his homemade gifts. The boys were presented with a scooter, refurbished ice skates, a pair of skis, and a brand new sled. The scrap parts in the barn had yielded some amazing gifts. Justin had a small wagon he used immediately to give his stuffed lamb a ride around the living room. Georgette and Elizabeth and Emily each had a small wooden jewelry box complete with lining. Raymond Sr. had also fashioned a handlebar basket for Justin's tricycle.

Everybody had everything they could ever have wished for. Justin sat his own fanny into his wagon and cuddled his lamb. His gaze was at an ideal angle to see a package under the tree. There it was. Again it had been pushed back under the tree so far only Justin from his low advantage point, could see it. But Justin did see it. He jumped up from his wagon seat and belly crawled under the tree to grab it and drag it into the middle of the parlor floor.

"Elizabeth," he yelled as he waved the Ladies' Auxiliary gift box again over his head, "Please unwrap this gift."

Elizabeth took the gift and checked the tag again. "'To Elizabeth-Open any time before Christmas.' Seems we didn't follow those instructions well."

Elizabeth looked to her mom for approval, "Sure, dear, open that one too."

Elizabeth unsleeved the card from its envelope, opened the gift card that was enclosed inside and read with widening eyes. She gave a curious look to Justin.

Georgette couldn't stand not knowing what was going on, " Read it to us honey."

She glanced at Justin again and read, "From Justin and the Baby Jesus."

Justin looked very surprised, as did everyone else, "From me?"

Elizabeth pointed to the card and said, "That's what it says here."

Justin took the card as Elizabeth ripped into the package. She parted the tissue to reveal a brand new pair of shoes. Tears welled up in her eyes. "How did they know?" she wondered out loud as she guessed that the Ladies' Auxiliary had a hand in this somehow.

Justin was doing his toad impression again but then immediately stopped jumping. He was confused by Elizabeth's choice of words. "They who?"

Elizabeth stopped herself; "Do you know who gave me this gift, Justin?"

"Yes, the Baby Jesus," and with that Justin started jumping again.

Georgette's forehead was furrowed again, confused, just trying to understand her youngest child. "But the card says that it is also from you Justin."

Justin came to his defense and stopped jumping afraid that he was in some kind of trouble, "Oh I just *asked* Him for the shoes. Baby Jesus must have done the shopping."

Elizabeth giggled at her brother and smiled at her mother. ~~Elizabeth pulled the wrapping eagerly apart. She lifted the lid from the box and put it aside. Gently she peeled back the tissue from the obvious pair of shoes that were nestled in the box.~~ Her face beamed as she pulled the first shoe into view. For there, before her eyes were the very same pair of shoes that she and her aunt had placed on order during their shopping sprees.

With abandon she grabbed the shoes out of the box and quickly slipped them on. "They fit perfectly and so beauti-

ful too." She ran to Justin and swooshed him up in her
arms. "Thank you, Sweetie!"

"Don't forget to thank Baby Jesus too!" Justin added as
she spun him until he giggled.

"Oh... He will be thanked in my nightly prayers little
fellow, but not just for the shoes. Mostly for giving me a
baby brother like you. Merry Christmas, Justin. Merry
Christmas and Thank you!" With that she kissed him and
danced around the room. Never again would she anticipate
Christmas for the getting. It had now become her season of
giving.

The Ladies' Auxiliary meeting was in full swing. Emma
Lou and Ida led ten other ladies during their weekly meeting. A dozen little church biddies clucked over their holiday basket success. They would settle their accounts and
plan their activities for the New Year. Ida tried to give her
end-of-year report but Emma Lou interrupted her, much to
Ida's disgust.

"We have $142.61 left in the treasury after delivering
ten baskets to five needy families," Ida started in her most
official tone.

"Each family received a Thanksgiving and Christmas
basket," added Emma, and Ida shot a "Don't tread on me"
look right through Emma and tried to regain control.

"We learned a few things to pass on to those who might
make deliveries in the future."

"NO LIVE TURKEYS!" shouted Emma, totally out of
control. One biddy turned to whisper to another.

"Is she drinking?"

The other lady gave her a horrified look and shook it off as the most terrible thought ever.

Ida was trying to control a building rage toward Emma for this disruptive behavior.

"Absolutely. No live turkeys...and..."

"And find a good driver," Emma wildly added.

Ida tried to say her piece again, "Excuse me!" At that point the meeting deteriorated into a sister-rivalry revival. Some of the church biddies took sides with one Snodgrass sister over the other and a near brawl ensued. There's something to be said about meaning well even if it is not always the result.

Uncle Howard and Aunt Emily's car pulled out of the driveway and onto the road. Watching them drive away, Raymond Sr., who rarely spoke, waxed poetic as he waved good-bye.

"May all your Christmas miles be paved with good intentions."

Justin added, "And guided by the twinkle of a Christmas star." The father and son stared at one another, each disbelieving the depth of the words uttered by the other.

Elizabeth hugged her lamb with one arm and Justin with the other as she watched her aunt and uncle's car drive toward the night horizon. A Christmas star twinkled down on her and Elizabeth winked back. The star's light reflected on Elizabeth's new shoes.

Justin saw his face as well as the reflected starlight in her shoes. "Have you ever talked to a star?"

"No, but I've listened a few times."

"Me, too!"

Justin felt the warmth of Christmas in the squeeze of his sister's hand. He had been able to be a Santa this year for the first time and he took this starlit moment to be thankful for that feeling as the star twinkled its acknowledgment and he gazed into the shine of Elizabeth's new shoes.

"Thank you, Baby Jesus." He paused to let his prayer have some delivery time and then said, "Ya know, Elizabeth?"

"No, what, Justin?"

"Being a Santa is maybe more fun than getting Santa's gifts."

"You are s-o-o-o right. How old are you?" She grabbed him up in her arms and he wrapped his legs around her like a little spider monkey. She carried him out of the cold and into the warmth of the farm's kitchen hearth.

Merry Christmas!

Epilogue

So much of this story is just plain fiction. I wasn't even born yet when the Christmas of 1939 happened to the world. My totally fictional characters like Emma Lou and Ida helped define a caring community and church family that certainly helped my mother's family survive a very difficult time.

Yet among the tall tales, there are scraps of my family's oral history. My mom, Elizabeth, did have a pet lamb that loved to jump rope. My mom still won't eat lamb. People usually don't eat any species that they have raised for companionship. I don't eat cats or dogs, either, so I honor her choice.

My mother, was convinced by her mother to go with an aunt and uncle and spend a whole week away from her family in order to give her brothers a used bike for Christmas. The escalator and revolving-door incidents really happened but the dress was pure fantasy. Mom did need a new pair of shoes but that was probably every Christmas since kids would grow out of stuff back then just like they do today.

Frog legs still remain a tasty treat, according to Mom. An opinion I share—must be some of that French (Alsacian) blood we have.

Certain family members reportedly refused to give my grandmother breakfast leftovers from their well-stocked pantry to feed my mom and uncles. One night my mother remembers having nothing for supper but one handful of popcorn. It was the Depression and hard times were felt by many.

My uncles were a crazy, nutty bunch of guys. One uncle turned into an electrician/inventor and ran a successful small business. He had a crazy laugh that all of my cousins worked hard to mimic. His nickname is still "Haw Haw" because of his outrageous laugh.

Two other uncles raced stock cars for years until a tragic collision convinced them both to initially stop. While this vaccine took in one uncle's case, the other just couldn't give up racing. He died at the age of forty-two during a race collision, while his wife was watching in the stands. This was the first uncle I ever said good-bye to. Another of the brothers passed away over the last few years. My uncle Justin and Mom are still as close as ever. He helps her around the house a lot. Often she has mentioned that Justin's handyman talents have assisted in keeping her place intact.

My granddad did lose part of his hand in a thrashing accident during the Depression. He reportedly made an impressive recovery. In my mom's words, "It was amazing what he could do with that hand."

Mom turned seventy-five at the end of July 2002. As part of her gift she was given a draft copy of "her story." I remember one year that Mom had entered a version of this very story into a short-story contest. But alas, she did not win.

That brings us to the childless aunt and uncle who treated my mother's family so well. They adopted two children, one boy and one girl. These two children were dearly loved, as you know they would be. These two sweet people raised a successful civil engineer son and a daughter about whose fate we seem to have no further information. The legacy of love and generosity that my mother's aunt and uncle showed my mother's family, I am sure did not stop with the Christmas of 1939.

I hope that the episodes written here help to not only preserve some of my family's oral history and legacy but also serve to entertain. If my uncles were anything, they were entertaining.

May God be with you all. A blessing I'm sure that I can extend from all three generations of Tiffin Columbian High School graduates.

My grandmother—class of 1915.

My mother—class of 1946.

Ms. Jenny Christine Deason—class of 1970.

New Shoes for Elizabeth

My given name is Jeanette, but only my grandmother, Georgette, could get away with calling me that. It's Jenny to the rest of the world. Remember, she didn't believe in nicknames. I was formerly Jenny Deason Tichenor until I recently reverted to my maiden name to honor my deceased father, Virgil Deason (1928-1987).

Merry Christmas,
"Jenny" Christine Deason
July 31, 2002
West Bloomfield, MI

Acknowledgments

Thanks to Charles P. Copeland for your undying belief that the book was worth the effort. Thank you also for reading it and finding all the factual mistakes about the autos and devices of the 1930s.

Derrick Deason Tichenor for the encouragement and love of a son, even when I was squirrely.

Noel Angelique Tichenor for the gentle input that only the sweet daughter that you are, would give. Thanks too for reading the book and finding all the snags my eyes could no longer see.

Thanks also to the folks of the Cingular Wireless amateur writers group, Heather, Bob, Linda, and Nancy. You made me laugh and that is worth the world. Thanks especially to Terri for reading the book and brainstorming a new ending with me.

Thanks to Terri and Heather for the WEB site work. My two girl friend geeks did a super job.

Thanks to Jennifer Dixon, my editor, who also gave me guidance and encouragement.

Thanks also to sister Amy and friend Denise who read the book and gave input. Bless you both for your time and kindly suggestions.

Thanks to the folks along the way that somehow steered me into following the light that led to this particular path. God Bless you all.

About the Author

Jeanette Christine Deason was born, the second in a family of four daughters, in the county seat of Seneca, Ohio. Tiffin is a college town, a town with two colleges yet with less than twenty thousand inhabitants. Jenny now lives in West Bloomfield, Michigan, with the love of her life, Charles. For most of the last three decades she has claimed Michigan as her home state.

Tiffin, Ohio, however, was a great place to grow up. It is a town filled with decent hard-working folks and many fond memories were created there. Graduating from Tiffin Columbian High School in 1970, Jenny then graduated from the University of Toledo, Ohio, in 1972. Upon entering graduate school at the University of Toledo, she went directly into a PhD psychology program, focusing on child development research. She then transferred to the University of Louisville to work on a master's degree in neuropsychopharmacology. In 1975 she began work for the old

Bell system as an engineer trainee and has been working in the network organization of the Baby Bells and spin-off cellular companies for the last twenty-five years. This included almost a year of work in Brussels, Belgium during the late 1990s.

Jenny is a mother of two now-grown children. She has successfully raised a daughter, Noel, who is a physical therapist in Portland, Oregon, and a son, Derrick Tichenor, who is the assistant manager of a pet store in the southeast Michigan area.

Jenny hopes to be a writer when she grows up and is a published poet. Jenny also enjoys writing screenplays, illustrates her poetry with cloud angel watercolors, and has written an album's worth of new Christmas carols. She simply loves the celebration of Christmas and hopes that this book assists in getting you in the spirit of the season.